FALLING DOWN

By David T. Boyd

(Second Edition)

TM

Another Shore Press, LLC

www.anothershorepress.com

FALLING DOWN (Second Edition)
Copyright © 2011 by David T Boyd

Edited by: Rolf Wolff
Cover Design by: David P. Schafer

Published by:
Another Shore Press, LLC
PO Box 381030
Brooklyn, New York 11238
www.anothershorepress.com

ISBN: 978-0-9832484-2-2

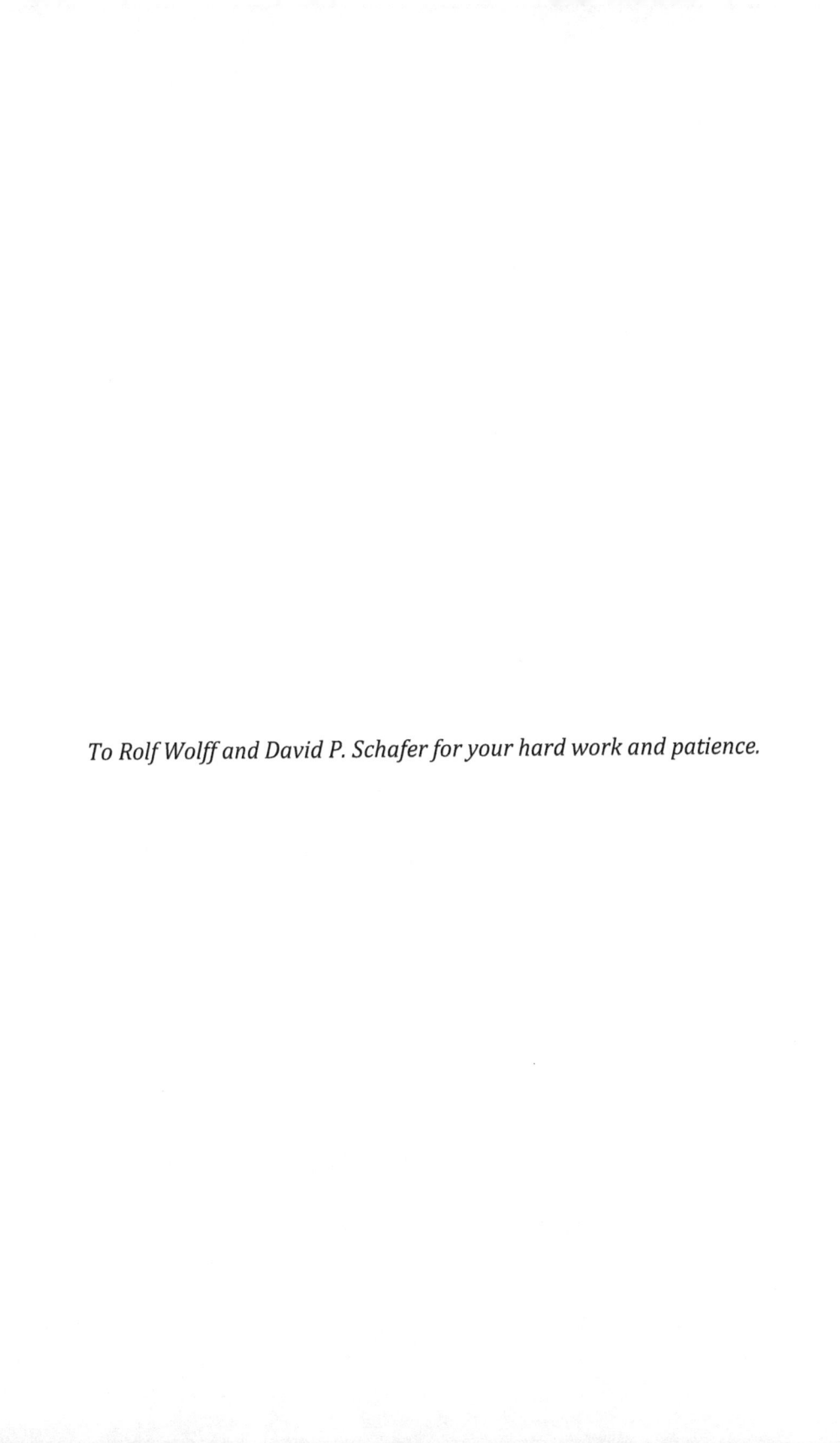

To Rolf Wolff and David P. Schafer for your hard work and patience.

Prologue

Father's Day, 2004

My life is filled with so many memories of days long since gone. They say it takes a few years for the memory of a child to develop beyond a blur of spotty moments, but mine is graced with placid thoughts of growing up on Longwood Drive in my hometown of Erie, Pennsylvania.

I recall fun-filled days of playing with the other kids in my neighborhood. Catching fireflies, or "lightning bugs" as we called them, was the thing to do during the summer months. Block club parties, little league baseball games - these and so much more remind me of what life was like back in the 1970s.

Janet Wilson, my mother, loved to make special things for me when I did well in school. Once she made my favorite dessert when I brought home straight A's on my report card. She baked a raspberry cheesecake, New York style of course, which she made from scratch. There was no greater incentive to keep my grades up than cheesecake, and I recall making myself sick because I ate the entire thing in one sitting. I didn't care; it only made me want it more.

"David, you eat enough for me and your father twice over" she used to say. My mother meant so much to me, so surely you can imagine it hurts to think that now she's gone – taken away from me forever. I miss her everyday.

My father? I'm not sure what to say about him, for he was such a driven, yet successful man. I'd never met anyone more ensconced in their profession than him. Many respected my father, saying "Mike Wilson was one of the brightest minds in psychiatry since Sigmund Freud." Though I found that to be a bit far fetched, he was a great man, one I admired yet felt some anger towards because I felt he didn't try hard enough in my younger years to get to know me, his only son.

At times I used to talk to him - long sentences, you know - and he would stare right at me and not hear a thing. He never really paid me much mind, but somewhere inside him I knew he loved me. He had to; after all, who couldn't love their own child?

Though scarce in nature, we did have our fleeting moments of father-son bonding. On occasion he'd drive us to Philadelphia to watch 76er games, back when Julius Erving was on the team. I loved those classic match-ups from back in the day, and the Sixers vs. the Boston Celtics were among the best ever. We even got tickets to see them win the 1983 NBA Championship back when the arena was called the Spectrum. Now I think they've changed the name to the Wachovia Center - more corporate bullshit if you ask me.

Shortly after mother passed away, things began to change for the better between my father and me. Eventually he met another woman, and though I wasn't keen on him meeting someone closer to my own age, she did seem nice and helped bridge the gap between the two of us.

These memories I will take with me because they're all I have right now. Though my father is still alive I look at him these days and find a shell of the person I once knew. He'd completely fallen down. For most of his life he remained in terrific shape, even as he entered into his fifties. All the exercising, eating the right foods – heck, at his age he could still give me a run for my money in a pick-up game of basketball. Now he looks so old, so hollow; I hardly see the person who at one time had it all together.

2

Even as I stand in this padded room looking at my father, curled up in a corner and lying on the floor, it still boggles my mind. He's been in the Smith Grove Sanitarium in Smith Grove, Illinois now for about three years; ever since...well...it's still so hard to believe!

What in the world would make my father commit murder?

How they found him, holding a knife all covered in blood in the foyer of his house – it's all so strange. As much as I don't know about my father, I can easily say he'd never do such a horrible thing.

The sad part is he hasn't spoken a word in years. All he does is rock back and forth, looking straight up into the air with his mouth wide open.

Sometimes I can hear him mumbling, but can't understand what he's trying to say. Hours and hours, every visit, that's what I see. Even when I look into his eyes, there's something there that tells me he's no murderer. I know I'm not wrong.

Strangely enough my father looked at me and tried to speak, but as before all that came out was gibberish. However, this was the first time he and I made eye contact in years, so naturally you can understand me being excited.

"Dad, please tell me what you see! I need to know so I can help you!"

He grabbed my coat, his brown eyes glaring directly into mine, trying desperately to tell his story.

"What is it dad? What are you trying to say?"

If only his eyes could talk, what would they tell me right now?

Chapter One: Phantasm

October 1, 1998

Distant thunder rumbled outside, becoming louder with each passing moment. Following the booming noise was a flash of lightning, momentarily brightening the sleepy town of Erie, Pennsylvania.

The wind accompanied the rain with its high shrill as the storm grew worse, making it difficult for anyone caught in Mother Nature's wrath to remain dry. Trees swayed back and forth and leaves flew everywhere, indiscriminately matting onto anything in its path. The few cars that drove past 115 Longwood Drive, the home of Mike and Janet Wilson, proceeded slowly for fear of having an accident along the road.

The clock at the town hall began its announcement that the midnight hour was at hand, ringing in the first moments of Thursday, October 1st, 1998. Despite the typhoon-like weather blowing around outside, most of the residents of Longwood Drive were tightly snug in their beds, paying the storm no mind, all except for Janet Wilson.

She was in the middle of a terrible nightmare, one that had plagued her slumber for the past two weeks. She'd tossed

4

and turned in bed for nearly fifteen minutes, only to wake to the sound of her grandfather clock in the hallway.

Janet sat up, breathing heavily and drenched in sweat, hearing a deafening sound - one louder than the thunder outside. She clutched her chest as the sound got even louder.

Thump, Thump! Thump, Thump!

It was the sound of her heart.

Janet threw aside the covers and stumbled into the master bathroom, slamming open the medicine cabinet. She ravaged through various bottles in a frantic search for her medication.

Not long ago Janet suffered a mild heart attack and was searching for her bottle of Xanax, which she took daily to help ease her anxiety attacks. Both of her adoptive parents had passed away, her father as recently as April due to cardiac arrest, brought on primarily by years of bad dieting and an excessive smoking habit.

Because of the stress from his death, as well as work-related issues, her health had continued to get worse, and these horrible dreams were not helping matters at all.

Janet continued to tear apart the cabinet for her medication.

"Where the fuck are they?" she thought.

Thump, Thump! Thump, Thump!

Janet found the bottle marked "Xanax" and quickly flipped open the cap, letting it drop as she continued her frenetic pace, pouring some water into a paper Dixie cup. After a huge gulp, she took a series of deep breaths, whispering to herself that everything would be fine.

The sound of her heart grew faint, her body finally becoming calm once again. Janet enjoyed the moment of silence and stood over the sink, watching beads of sweat from her forehead drip into the drain, the sound echoing from the tiled bathroom walls.

She took a deep breath, bent down and collected the Dixie cups she'd scattered across the floor. As she closed the medicine cabinet, the mirror revealed a large, hulking man dressed in a black parka and ski mask standing behind her. An angry, bloody gash oozing between his eyes; he appeared to have been shot in the head.

The Man in Black reached out and grabbed Janet, swinging her around.

"Please don't kill me!" she pleaded, dropping the Dixie cups on the floor a second time.

"Janet! It's me, it's Mike!"

She realized who it was and stopped her struggle, sobbing in his arms for several minutes.

***

After Janet managed to calm down, they walked to the bedroom. Mike sat her down on the edge of their king-sized bed, kneeling before her, tenderly kissing her hand.

"What's wrong honey, another bad dream?"

"It's the same dream over and over again, but...it sort of...*changed* this time around."

"How so?"

"Well," she began, "it started the same way. We were in bed, and in the middle of the night I awoke because of a horrible thunderstorm. I heard a noise downstairs and couldn't wake you, so I decided to check it out myself. I went to the closet and got a gun, then crept quietly down the steps where that man in black was stealing some of our things."

Janet paused, giving herself a moment to collect her thoughts. After taking a deep breath, she continued.

"He was walking around whistling that old nursery rhyme 'London Bridge is Falling Down,' and must've heard me approaching him. He had a knife and came after me, but I shot him in the face...but he kept coming at me, getting closer and closer."

Tears began to form in Janet's eyes as she looked directly at Mike.

"This time he actually caught me! I woke up just as his knife went into my chest. Oh Mike, I was so scared!"

"There, there now, honey," Mike said, reassuringly, "why don't you get some rest. Call the office in the morning and tell them you'll be working from home. You really should try and relax."

"I can't. I've got that Jefferson case up for trial next week, and...."

"Ah, ah now," Mike interrupted, "don't argue with the doctor!"

He gently caressed her hand.

"Okay, I won't argue. In fact, I'm going back to bed right now."

"That's my baby," he said, smiling.

Mike kissed her on the forehead and laid her back in bed, covering her up. He stood there a moment with a huge smile on his face.

"Love you, sweetie," he whispered.

"Love you too."

Mike climbed into bed and, after taking one last look at her, turned over and quickly fell into a deep sleep.

Janet tried to do the same, but found it difficult – understandably so! She lay in bed listening to the harsh winds and the loud clapping of thunder that caused a chill to run down her spine. She closed her eyes, only to see flashes of that tall man in her dreams coming after her.

Janet's imagination began to play tricks as she looked around the room. In the darkness she could swear the clothes hanging in her open closet resembled rows of ghosts hovering gently in mid-air, and after a short while all she could do was stare outside as the wind blew leaves and broken branches against the window.

Chapter Two: The Mirror

As she lay in bed, Janet looked at her dresser drawer in the right-hand corner of their room. With each flash of lightning she could see glimpses of a handheld mirror that had been given to her many years ago as a child.

Her face slowly changed from a look of anxiousness to the makings of a smile. She remembered the day the mirror was given to her.

It was on her seventh birthday.

***

May 19, 1951

Janet recalled the day being very cold and rainy in North Philadelphia as she rode home with her classmates on the school bus. She sat near the front, chatting with some of her friends, and as she was in the middle of eating a chocolate candy bar the bus driver slammed on his brakes.

Many of the children were thrown against the seat in front of them, and Janet's head hit the back of the bus drivers' chair. She also mashed the chocolate bar against her white blouse, squeezing it between her fingers.

Once the bus came to a complete stop the children were all reaching under their seats for pencils, crayons, books and whatever else had fallen out of their backpacks.

Janet began licking her fingers clean of the chocolate.

"Goddamn bitch!" the bus driver shouted rather emphatically. The children snickered at him for cursing. The bus driver remembered where he was and his face turned bright red.

Janet stood very slowly and looked over the driver's right shoulder, the outline of her brown hair with pigtails and white barrettes gradually becoming more and more in view.

Standing perfectly still in front of the bus was a woman dressed entirely in black, wearing a long parka and matching dress that rested just below her knees. She had the hood of the parka over her head to keep her hair dry, but it was so far over her face it cast a dark shadow over most of her features. All you could see was the bottom of her nose, lips and jaw line, in addition to long strands of jet-black hair matted along her cheeks because of the rain.

She wore white socks and black Converse sneakers, and carried a large shopping bag, with a backpack thrown over her shoulders. She appeared homeless, though her clothing looked relatively new.

The mystery woman continued to stand perfectly still, then tilted her head as Janet appeared from behind the driver, approaching the windshield of the school bus.

"Get out of my way, you old hag!" the bus driver screamed, frantically motioning his hands from left to right. The second outburst caused the children to snicker once again.

The woman smiled and waved. The bus driver promptly responded by flipping her 'the bird' as she began walking slowly down the crosswalk, eyes still focused on the windshield. The driver grumbled something about 'silly dames' and started the bus, while Janet continued focusing her attention on the woman, who appeared to be waving directly at her. She returned the favor, looking out the window until the bus pulled away and the woman faded from view.

A short time later Janet arrived home, where her mother, Margaret Hampton, welcomed her at the front door with hugs and kisses. Margaret knelt down and began removing her white shoes. Her father, Ted, was still at work.

9

"Happy birthday Pumpkin!" Margaret said, giving her a great big kiss.

She glanced at Janet's blouse, and attempted to touch the smeared chocolate, then looked into her daughter's eyes once again.

"What happened here?"

"I had a boo-boo," Janet said, looking at her mother with puppy dog eyes.

"All right, I don't want to know," Margaret replied, shaking her head. "By the way, I have something very special for you."

"Really?" Janet said, the excitement obvious in her voice.

"Uh huh, and it's upstairs in your room."

"Yay!"

Janet ran up the stairs and into her room to find a hand held mirror sitting on her bed. On the back of the mirror was a design of a woman hovering gracefully in the heavens, with her arms outstretched and draped clothing that appeared to float gently in the air.

Though it appeared to be a religious piece, the woman had a troubled look on her face. Her clothing seemed to match her mood. Instead of being dressed in white or gold, she wore black as if she were in mourning.

The woman was looking down at an infant dressed in white, resting peacefully on a small cloud. Gathered around the infant were two guardian angels, one male and one female, and they appeared to be attending to the infant's needs.

The sight of this odd gift caused Janet to frown. She'd hoped it would be a toy, or perhaps some candy. Instead all she got was this ugly mirror.

"What's this?" she asked her mom, who was standing in the doorway.

"It's a mirror, Pumpkin. But it's not just any mirror. It's a magical one that has the power to reveal a beautiful little girl every time you look into it."

"What beautiful little girl would that be?" queried Janet, knowing she asked a loaded question.

"I think you know the answer to that one, you silly thing. I hope you like it Pumpkin, for it was given to you by someone who loves you very much."

After hearing her mother's explanation, Janet's mood changed quickly. She loved her parents very much, and for a child she seemed to be quite intuitive for her age. The fact that this mirror was from someone who loved her meant more than the gift itself. Because of this she was a very agreeable and easy to please. She understood the importance of giving at an early age, quite an unusual trait for a child to have.

"Oh mommy, I love it!" Janet said, grinning from ear to ear.

She kissed her mother on the cheek, and together they peered into the mirror.

Chapter Three: Regina

Janet couldn't help but smile as she lay in bed, looking in the direction of her mirror. She believed all her birthdays were special in one way or another, but she was particularly fond of number seven because of the mirror, which she'd kept in excellent condition after all of these years.

As the thunder continued to rumble, a bright light entered her bedroom. Thinking it was the lightning, Janet didn't make much of it, until she realized the light wasn't coming from the outside, but from her dresser.

She got up from bed and walked slowly toward the mirror, grabbing its handle, remembering the tingly sensation she felt whenever she picked it up - a sensation that lasts even today.

After cautiously peering into the oval face, a silhouette of a young girl standing in front of what appeared to be a sunrise began taking form. Once the complete image appeared Janet realized it was her imaginary childhood friend "Regina."

Regina was wearing a light blue blouse, her hair done in braids with matching blue barrettes at the ends. As a child Regina was Janet's best friend, and they often sat for hours talking to one another through that very same mirror. The girls told each other everything, played together, dressed up in the same clothes. They even *looked* like each other, for she saw Regina as the sister that she never had.

For most of her life, Janet was basically a loner as a child. It grew worse when she was told she'd been adopted, and though her parents loved her very much, and she adored them, she always felt like a part of her was missing because she didn't know anything about her real mom and dad. All she had was Regina, and until now they hadn't spoken since Janet was thirteen years old.

Janet smiled at the thought of seeing Regina again, though she looked the same as she did when they were kids.

"Hey silly-nilly," Regina said, smiling wide. "Remember me?"

As kids they called each other "silly-nilly" and "girly whirly".

"Hey girly-whirly! "It's been so long...where have you been? I've really missed you!"

"You'll never guess what!" Regina said. "I've got a great big surprise for you."

"What is it?" Janet asked, eagerly wanting to know.

"Well if I told you it wouldn't be a surprise now would it, goofy?" Regina cackled. "I'll show you though, real soon."

The light from the mirror began to fade.

"Regina...Regina wait!" Janet said, grabbing the mirror.

"Later silly-nilly." Regina's image faded away.

Mike head propped up from the pillow. He was clearly half-asleep, frantically scanning the room, unaware that Janet was standing in front of the bed.

"Wha...huh...aw momma, I don't wanna go to school," he groaned.

Janet snickered. "Go back to sleep sonny, and I'll put a special treat in your lunch box for you."

"Oh goody," Mike said, half-smiling with his eyes still closed. His head flopped back onto the pillow and was quickly asleep once again.

***

Janet slid into bed with her incoherent husband, thinking of her and Regina's conversations from their childhood days.

She remembered being eleven years old, hearing her mother and father argue in their bedroom for the first time. Her father had just come home from a tough day at the office and sounded as if he'd been drinking.

Ted spent nearly three months as the lead prosecutor on a murder case, which he ended up losing that afternoon. Not being the type of person that took losses well, he came home and, for the first and only time, took it out on her mother. Janet had never heard her father so angry in her life, and his voice - in addition to the booze that flowed through his veins - made him sound like a monster.

She grabbed her mirror and called on Regina, who immediately came to the rescue.

"What's wrong girly-whirly?" Regina asked.

"It's mommy and daddy," Janet replied. "They're fighting really, really loud. They're scaring me!"

Regina could easily tell that Janet was very afraid. In the background Janet heard Ted's voice getting louder in an outburst that surprised even Margaret. The two of them continued arguing as the girls spoke to one another.

"Why is he yelling like that?" Janet begged. "Why doesn't he stop it?"

"Now you calm down, girly-whirly!" Regina said, convincingly. "I don't think your daddy means to frighten you. He's probably just real mad right now. Remember what you did the last time you got real mad?"

"Yeah, I do," said Janet. "I tore up my favorite Barbie doll."

"See?" Regina replied. "That's all your daddy is doing right now. He's tearing up his favorite doll. But when he stops and looks at what he did he'll be sorry. He's not mean to you or your mommy! Don't worry, I'll bet he won't do it ever again."

"You think so?" Janet said.

"I *know* so!"

Regina was right.

14

The very next morning Janet came to the kitchen to find her father wearing a pair of shorts and a tee shirt that said *#1 Dad*, the same shirt that Janet picked out for him last Father's Day.

He also wore an apron, and from the aroma of sausage that filled the kitchen he appeared to be cooking breakfast. There were fresh cut roses on the table for both her and her mother. Both parents were sitting at the table and Margaret was holding his hand as he gazed tenderly into her eyes. His attention was diverted as Janet entered the kitchen.

"I'm sorry for the way I was last night Pumpkin," Ted said, somberly. "Do you forgive your daddy?"

Without saying a word Janet rushed up and hugged her father tenderly. He began to cry, and he reached out with his right hand, stroking his wife's face. The three of them sat there for what appeared to be hours, bonding together again as father, mother and child.

***

Janet finally overcame the terror of the night and fell peacefully back to sleep, finding solace in the memories of her family and Regina.

Suddenly the storm was over.

Chapter Four: The Visitor

The next day began on a pleasant note. The puddles from last night's storm were slowly beginning to dry, as the sun shined through Janet's living room window.

People in the neighborhood made their way to their front porches for the morning paper, noting some of the remnants of last night's activities. A few were surprised at how heavily the storm came down, for their cars and walkways were covered with leaves and branches. The weather was perfect for taking a walk in the park, sitting outside and reading a good book, or perhaps to simply sleep in the comforts of a brisk autumn morning.

Janet awoke in better spirits and was in the kitchen fixing breakfast at eight o'clock as Mike came downstairs dressed for work. Known for his strict attention to detail, especially regarding his wardrobe, he wore a Hickey Freeman suit, Church's traditional brown cap toe shoes, argyle socks, a perfectly starched Sea Island cotton white shirt, and a navy-gold bar stripe tie. He carried a maroon leather briefcase, and the aroma of Tommy Hilfiger after-shave, which Janet loves, announced his entrance into the kitchen.

Though Mike has a full beard, he kept it neat by shaving every morning, giving himself a splash of Tommy for good measure. He greeted his wife with a kiss on the cheek as she stood over the stove.

"I love the smell of a Tommy Man," Janet said, returning his kiss.

"I wear it just for you dear," he replied. "And how are *you* this morning? Feeling better?"

"A little bit, but I'm still very tired. I guess the office can do without me for a day."

"That's my baby," he said. "Relax today, and when I get home this evening I'll take you anywhere you want to go, all right?"

"Sounds perfect," Janet replied.

She gave him another kiss, this time it was much more passionate.

"Boy, you're cooking in more ways than one," he said, smiling, as he pulled up a chair at the kitchen table.

Janet placed a hearty plate of pancakes, eggs and sausage links in front of him, followed by a tall glass of grapefruit juice. Mike sampled his food, nodding his head in appreciation.

"Nobody burns in the kitchen like you, babe." To *burn* was slang for *cook*, which was his way of saying she's the best.

"A great breakfast for a great man," Janet replied, reaching over and gently touching his face. She gave him another kiss.

***

They sat at the kitchen table looking deeply into one another's eyes, speaking in ways that words could never express. In Janet's mind, they were soul mates, having lived through so much in their thirty-two years of marriage. From the time they met at the University of Illinois at Urbana-Champaign until the present, the two of them remained together and very much in love.

Janet became pregnant with their son David while in law school, but fortunately Margaret was able to assist as they completed their post-graduate studies. A tenacious attorney in her own right, Janet built a solid reputation as a prosecutor in

17

the district attorney's office and was rewarded with a high paying job at Jamison, Boyer and Johnson Law Offices in Philadelphia, where she made the transformation into a successful defense attorney.

After finishing medical school, Mike completed his residency and found a job at Saint Thomas Aquinas Hospital in Erie, where Janet eventually opened her own law practice. David, now age twenty-eight, is a first year MBA student at Northwestern University in Evanston, Illinois.

It took some time for both of them to build what they now had, but it was well worth the wait. Thirty-two years of marriage and they couldn't be happier.

***

Janet was still looking into his eyes for what seemed like hours when she finally spoke: "You're welcome."

"But I didn't say thank you," Mike replied. He had a dazed look on his face, similar to the one last night when Janet was talking to Regina.

"Yes you did," she said, tapping his nose. "You'd better eat before your food gets cold."

"Eat what?" Mike said, still looking dazed. Janet smacked his thigh.

"You silly boy," she said.

Mike smiled and continued eating. Upon completion of his delicious meal, he assisted Janet in cleaning the dishes and wiping off the kitchen table. He washed his hands, then scooped up his briefcase and grabbed Janet from behind as she was wiping the counter tops.

"So what are you going to do with your day?" he asked.

"Well, I've got my appointment with Dr. Martin today," she said.

"Oh yes, eleven-thirty, right?"

"Yep," Janet replied.

"Why not come to my office at the medical center and have lunch?" Mike said. "My treat for the girl playing hooky! Tell 'ole Bill if he's got a moment and wants to tag along, he can."

"I can have lunch with *two* good-looking men? I can't pass up an opportunity like that."

"Great. Come over at twelve-thirty and I'll see you then," he replied.

Mike entered the garage through an entryway in the foyer, closing the door behind him. Janet could hear the car start and the garage door lift up. She walked out to the living room and stood by the window, watching Mike's Lexus ES300 back out of the driveway and into the street. He honked the horn and quickly made his way down the block.

Janet returned to finish her cleanup, collecting the used dishtowels and placing them into their dumbwaiter at the far corner of the kitchen. She watched as the towels began their descent to the laundry room, thinking how lucky they were to be blessed with such a beautiful home and family.

***

Mike and Janet bought their home twenty-five years ago in a nice area of Erie, along the southern edge of town. Purchased for about $165,000 in 1983, the house now valued over $1,500,000 given the appreciation and amount of work they put into it, and was recently described in the Erie Daily Times and Morning News as "Erie's most elegant Victorian home," with over four thousand square feet of living space.

There were four floors finished with a total of five bedrooms, three and a half baths, a living room and dining room, pantry, kitchen, parlor, family room, den, and a hot tub/exercise room. Janet had the dumbwaiter installed, which made it easier for transporting heavier objects around the house and doing laundry.

It was a smart real estate decision on their part. Ted and Margaret helped with the purchase of the house, as they gave the young couple a sizeable down payment as part of a belated wedding gift. At first Mike resisted, stating they should do it on their own. Secretly Janet thought Mike was embarrassed because his family was dirt-poor, but later he softened to the idea and eventually made good on a promise to pay them back, sending a check through the mail.

Ted tore up the check upon receipt and refused to accept a replacement. Though he was a wealthy man, he also was very generous.

***

Janet left the kitchen and decided to relax in the den, turning on the television and stretching out on her leather couch.

"Oprah's on!" she thought. "All right!"

After getting herself comfortable it wasn't long before Janet began to feel the effects of last night's lack of rest. A mere ten minutes later she drifted off to sleep, not realizing there was someone watching her from behind, standing outside the double doors that led to the deck. The figure was wearing a black parka, jeans and thick-soled black boots, as well as a pair of leather gloves. They also appeared to have a bag strapped over their right shoulder, and for the next few minutes continued to stand perfectly still by the doors – waiting to make their move.

Finally they unlocked the door with a key and quietly slid into the den, walking very slowly toward Janet, who was still asleep and unable to hear anything because of the television.

The mystery person carefully approached the couch when the side of the shoulder bag bumped into the end table, knocking over a family photo of Janet, Mike and David. The sound of the frame hitting the floor was loud enough to rouse Janet.

The figure watched, as Janet turned over in her sleep, unaware that someone else was in the room, and when she stopped moving the figure grabbed the picture off the floor and rested it on top of the end table. The figure reached inside the bag and pulled out a thin book, placing it on the coffee table, and after taking a quick glance at the TV, quietly backtracked through the double doors, locking them once again and disappearing from the deck.

Seconds later the telephone began to ring, stirring Janet from her nap. She fumbled around until she eventually located the phone and picked it up.

"Hello?" she mumbled.

"Hey sweetheart! Did I wake you?" The caller was Mike.

"Oh, no don't worry about it honey, I need to get up anyway," Janet yawned, "I have to get showered to go see the doctor."

Janet checked the clock on the wall, which read 9:45 AM.

"That's fine baby, I just wanted to make sure you were enjoying your morning off."

"You're sweet," she said, smiling, as she glanced over at the coffee table.

Janet noticed a book sitting on the table that she wasn't familiar with. She leaned forward and grabbed it, reading the title.

The cover said: "Brother Stern's Collection of Favorite Children's Nursery Rhymes."

Janet opened the book and looked at the table of contents. The book was full of illustrations featuring kids playing, reading and drawing. The artwork looked as if children, as opposed to a trained artist, had designed it.

Janet ran her finger down the list of nursery rhymes, fifty in total. Some of them were well known, like "Georgie Porgie" and "Little Bo Peep", while others were relatively unheard of.

After further examination, Janet saw a title circled in red ink; the sight of it caused her to gasp...it was London Bridge is Falling Down.

"Mike, did you leave this book for me to find?" Janet asked excitedly.

"What book, honey?"

"This nursery rhyme book. I woke up and it was sitting right here on the coffee table."

"Sweetie, how can I do that and be here at work? You saw me leave the house this morning."

A cold chill rushed through her.

"Mike, let me call you back!" she said, hanging up the phone without waiting for an answer.

Janet sat up, quickly scanning the room, her eyes resting on the double glass patio doors. She got up from the couch and slowly crept toward the doors, feeling the tension build in her chest. Through the glass she peered outside at her redecorated patio. All she saw were her matching tables and chairs, a few plants and a large charcoal barbecue grill. Janet recalled something Mike likes to say on a regular basis: "No gas grills in this house...not as long as I'm Mr. Barbeque of Erie!"

He can be so damn picky sometimes.

21

Janet unlocked the door and carefully opened it, hearing it creak as the opening became wider and wider. She looked to her right and stepped out onto the deck when she felt a hand touch her left wrist.

"Gotcha!" the man said, grabbing Janet.

Janet screamed and pulled away, falling backwards into the den.

"Janet, all you all right?" the man chuckled, leaning over her as she lay sprawled out on the floor.

It was her next-door neighbor Charlie.

"Charlie! I should've known it was you!" Janet said, relieved.

***

Charlie and Maria Richardson have lived next door to Mike and Janet since they moved into their house. The foursome are very close friends, however Janet and Mike have often found themselves the object of Charlie's many gags. Charlie owned a very successful toy and novelty store in downtown Erie that's become almost a staple of the community. He's been in business for many years after cutting his teeth as a door-to-door salesman for another novelty company based out of State College.

Charlie was successful because of hard work, and it was through his many pranks that he was able to keep his spirits up and maintain a positive attitude. He and his wife Maria raised the business from the ground up and developed it slowly into a multi-million dollar empire, selling thousands of toys and novelty gifts annually throughout North America and Europe. *The Gift of Gags* was the name of his business, but despite his success, Charlie continued to be the same old prankster he'd always been. At the ripe age of seventy, he figured why bother changing what works?

Despite his annoying gags Mike and Janet couldn't ask for better friends, travel companions and role models as to how to maintain a successful marriage. Charlie and Maria have been married for over forty-three years and have raised four children: Walter, Jonathan, Rachel and Charles, Jr., all of whom were part of the family business.

***

Charlie extended his hand, helping Janet from the floor.

"Charlie you scared the shit out of me!" She said, slapping his left shoulder.

"Hell girl, somebody's gotta make sure you're still alive and enjoying life, you know?" Charlie said, still snickering.

"Uh huh," Janet said, smiling at Charlie. "By the way Mr. Wisenheimer, did you happen to deliver this book to me while I was sleeping?"

Janet showed Charlie the book of nursery rhymes. He looked at the book and shook his head.

"Nope, never seen it before in my life. In fact, I came over to give you these."

Charlie reached in his back pocket and gave Janet a few items from today's mail.

"The damn mailman fucked up again. I keep tellin' that sum-bitch that I'm not as ugly as your husband, but he evidently doesn't seem to think so."

"Well wasn't that lovely of you to say?" Janet said, still smiling with a touch of sarcasm in her voice. "Can I offer you some coffee Charlie? I've got some already made in the kitchen."

"Hell no!" Charlie said. "The last thing I need in me is caffeine."

"On second thought, you're right. How about a glass of water?" Janet asked.

"Naw, I gotta get back to the store. I just stopped home because I forgot something and saw your mail sitting in my mailbox."

Charlie started towards the door, then turned back to say something else to Janet.

"Oh, by the way I saw someone wearing a black raincoat coming out of your backyard. That's another reason why I came over here - to check on you. You all right?"

Janet shuddered, remembering why she went to open the door in the first place. She also realized what it looked like with her being home unexpectedly and a mysterious stranger sneaking out the house after her husband left for work.

She walked closer to Charlie looking a bit nervous, thankfully patting his shoulder.

"Thanks Charlie, yes I'm fine," she said. "I think someone was in the house while I was taking a nap. I need to make sure I keep this place locked up tight. Lots of strange people lurking about!"

"All-rightie then! I came over here with my ass-kickin' boots in case anyone was over here that shouldn't be!"

Charlie picked up each foot, revealing a pair of very thick-soled black boots.

"You must've been prepared to kick a lot of ass Charlie!" Janet chuckled.

"Damn straight, girl, and be careful next time! Get yourself a Winchester and peel one off in someone's backside if they come around again," Charlie said, walking toward the double doors.

"Have a good one, and call us so me and the missus can have ya'll over for dinner Friday night."

"Will do Charlie, thanks," Janet replied. Charlie shut the doors, the sound of his boots becoming faint as he went back to his house.

Janet grabbed the telephone and dialed Mike's office number. After a few rings she heard Judy, Mike's receptionist, pick up the phone.

"Dr. Wilson's office, Judy speaking, how may I help you?"

"Hi Judy, its Janet Wilson calling, is my husband available?"

"Hi Mrs. Wilson, no I haven't seen the doctor all morning. He doesn't have an appointment until 10:30."

Janet seemed puzzled by that. She thought she heard Mike say he was at work when he called.

"Okay Judy, well tell him I'll be there for lunch, all right?"

"I sure will Mrs. Wilson, talk to you later."

Janet hung up the phone then sat on the couch, first looking at the book she found, then at the mail Charlie gave her. She noticed one of the letters had her name and address typed on the envelope, but there was no return address in the upper left corner. The envelope was postmarked for yesterday's date.

Her hands began to tremble, and as she opened the letter she could see words spelled from letters that appeared to be cut out of a magazine.

The note read: "Do you like your book Janet?"

Janet gasped.

She immediately grabbed the note and the book, walked outside and threw them into the trash. Turning around slowly she began looking for the culprit as she did earlier while heading back into the house, slamming and locking the patio doors behind her.

Her chest tightened as she began fretfully pacing in the den, trying to figure out what was happening. The last thing she needed was to become stressed before meeting with her cardiologist. In fact, one could dare say she needed that right now like she needed a heart attack.

Janet could hear her clock strike ten from the upstairs hallway, so she put aside the morning's events and rushed upstairs to get ready for her appointment, throwing clothes about as she made her way toward the shower.

As she hurriedly bathed under the water, the figure wearing the black parka and thick-soled boots returned to the patio and removed the book and letter from her trash can.

After all...they certainly couldn't leave evidence lying around, now could they?

Chapter Five: Elevator Trouble

Janet listened to people commenting on the radio about today's Oprah Winfrey Show while driving her vehicle. A long time Oprah fan, Janet has tuned in to her show for years. Oprah enthusiasts know she got her start as host on AM Chicago, a local morning TV talk show in the Chicago metro area back in the early 1980s.

Prior to Oprah's arrival, the show was only a half-hour, and brought in consistently low ratings. In less than a year, Ms. Winfrey turned it around, making it the hottest program in town.

Because of AM Chicago's success it eventually led to Oprah having her own hour-long show, and established her as a household name around the country and the world. Janet liked Oprah because she's such a strong, sexy, intelligent and business-minded woman – much like herself. She could identify with the upward mobility and confidence that Oprah presented to her viewers, and someday hoped to be able to see a taping of the show while visiting David at Northwestern.

"I just might do that," she thought, as she headed into the heart of town.

Janet entered a parking garage alongside the hospital and drove up to the third level. She masterfully parked her brand-new white Toyota 4-Runner into a parking space, shut off the ignition and sat quietly in her vehicle, noting a fluttering sound in her voice with each exhale. The activities of the morning had placed Janet on constant guard, and she found herself thoroughly scanning her rear view mirror before opening the driver side door.

She exited the vehicle, hearing the "chirping" sound from her keyless remote, and looked around the dimly-lit garage; the musty smell of dampness from the previous night's storm was so heavy you could cut it with a knife. Since there were so few spaces, she had to park farther away from the elevator than she desired. Janet preferred to park closer to exits in parking garages, mainly for safety reasons, but since she was running late there was no time to be very picky.

Janet began walking toward the elevator, and with each step she could hear the "click, clack" of her heels – the sound echoing all around her as if she were at the top of a canyon. She nervously scanned the area as she continued making her way across.

Janet heard steps behind her and turned to see a man standing in the shadows approximately a hundred feet away. They both stood perfectly still, opposite of each other, almost resembling a "high noon" showdown seen mostly in old, spaghetti westerns.

Janet was unable to see the man's face, but found it odd that he was merely standing there. As she turned to continue her walk, the man turned his head and reached into his pocket, pulling out something long and shiny in his right hand.

He quickly began walking towards her.

"Oh shit!"

Janet turned and made a mad dash towards the elevator. Once she approached the doors the panel indicated the elevator was on the first floor, and she was on the third. Janet began pounding the down button, turning to see that the man behind her had picked up his pace.

Thump, Thump! Thump, Thump!

Janet could feel her heart racing again. She briefly turned away and saw the elevator had risen to the second floor.

27

Looking behind her again, he was now half the distance away and closing fast!

Thump, Thump! Thump, Thump!

Ding! The sound announced the elevator approaching the third floor, and as the doors opened Janet quickly rushed inside, pressing the close button repeatedly. The stranger was now running at full speed with the object in his hand leading the way. She stumbled to the back of the elevator in a near frenzy. Just before the doors closed, a hand came through, stopping the elevator and the doors began to open again.

Thump, Thump! Thump, Thump!

Janet was in a total panic and blacked out, slumping to the floor of the elevator. The stranger knelt down, trying to revive her.

***

Sometime later Janet awoke rather startled, realizing she was in someone's office and lying on a leather couch. Dr. Martin and Marlene, his receptionist, were standing over her with concerned looks.

"Is she going to be all right?" Marlene asked, handing Janet a cup of water.

"Yes, she'll be fine," he replied. "Janet, I'm so sorry for scaring you like that."

"You?" Janet said, still a bit shaken up from the excitement.

She took a quick gulp of water, handing the cup back to Marlene, who left the two of them to talk.

"Yes, sad to say. I'm a cardiologist and I almost cause one of my patients to have a heart attack. That's not good for business."

Bill chuckled from the irony of his statement.

"What was that in your pocket?"

Bill reached over to his desk and presented a slender cellular phone for Janet to see.

"I almost smashed this while trying to stop the elevator from closing. This phone cost me a lot of money." he said.

"Oh...sorry Bill," Janet replied. Her face was turning red.

"That's okay. If you caused me to break it I'd just add the price of a new one to your bill," he quipped, returning his cell phone to the desk, his trademark evil grin intact.

Given Bill's massive size and knowing him to be a former All-American wrestler at Temple, that look would sometimes cause her to shudder. Janet couldn't always tell if he was kidding or there was more behind what he said than she cared to know. This time Janet took his comments in a joking manner and smiled for the first time since her breakfast with Mike.

"I'll have a nurse take you to the exam room once I'm ready. I shouldn't be more than a few minutes."

"Not a problem. I'll be right here."

Bill left his office, closing the door behind him. Janet could hear his footsteps going down the hallway as she stood, rubbing her hands and looking around the office.

The room was rather stuffy, so Janet opened the windows behind Bill's desk, letting in the cool brisk autumn air. She stepped back, taking in a deep breath, exhaling slowly. With each breath she began to feel better, as if a tremendous weight was lifted from her shoulders, and she looked over at the desk where the cell phone lay.

Her smile grew wider in remembrance of her recent scare, thinking how foolish she must've looked. Oh well – what better a person to pass out in front of than a cardiologist? Besides, there was no harm done.

Janet's eyes met the doctor's bookcase to the left of his desk. Upon the shelf rest a series of pictures taken over the years. There were shots of Bill as a young man in his wrestling uniform in high school and college; another of him standing next to his parents at his college graduation. On his filing cabinet in the corner was a picture of Mike and Bill standing next to each other, shaking hands and grinning from ear to ear.

"There goes that evil grin again," she thought.

Though the photo was taken well over a decade ago, the effect of it was something that caught Janet's attention to this day. She remembered that picture, since she was the one who had taken it. Mike was so excited to be finished with med school, and she recalled the boys going out and getting really drunk, with her approval of course. Janet called a limousine and had the driver take the two friends, as well as a few others from their class, any place they wanted for one evening. Mike worked very hard to maintain his grades and, along with Dr. Martin, graduated in the top five percent of his class as reward for his efforts, so allowing them to let off some steam seemed like a nice idea.

Janet never felt more proud of her husband than she did at that moment. That picture represented the very best of their successes together as man and wife, and Janet had that same portrait on her mantle over the fireplace at home.

"That's my baby," Janet whispered.

She picked up the picture and ran her finger across Mike's smiling face, then glanced across a few others on the bookshelf. There were several photos of Bill and his wife Madeline, along with their three children – two girls and one boy. Mike was the godfather of the boy, also named Mike – the youngest of the three. The girls were Kristen, who was the eldest, and Renee. All three had moved out of the house and were involved in their own lives. Kristen and Renee were both in graduate school; Kristen attended law school at Cornell University and Renee was in her first year at Harvard earning her MBA.

Mike was a third year cadet in the United States Naval Academy in Annapolis, Maryland. He'd recently returned to Erie, visiting his parents while on a semester break from his studies. Like his father, Mike was a very tall, solid young man who was on the wrestling team at the Academy.

Janet had a hard enough time accepting the fact that David was reaching his thirties. Now Bill's kids had also grown up quickly before her eyes.

"Where has the time gone," mused Janet. "I must really be getting old!"

Her attention returned once again to the picture she took. As her gaze took her deeper into Dr. Martin's a sudden noise made Janet jump, knocking over a few pictures from the shelf.

The shrieking noise came from the Bill's cell phone, which continued to chirp away as the nurse abruptly entered the doctor's office.

"Are you alright ma'am?" the nurse asked, looking at the scattered photos across the floor. The cell phone stopped ringing.

"Yes, I'm fine," Janet snapped. "You just startled me is all."

The nurse seemed to scoff at Janet, but regained her composure. She took a deep breath before she spoke.

"The doctor will see you now, please follow me."

The nurse gestured for her to enter the hallway, and after she straightened the mess she'd created, Janet picked up her purse and walked towards the door. Taking one last glance at his desk, she walked out of the office. The nurse followed closely behind, shaking her head, also taking a puzzled glance at the phone as well.

Chapter Six: To "J" with Love

The town bell rang announcing it was half past one in the afternoon. As it had this time yesterday, it appeared as if it were about to rain, for the morning sun disappeared behind a heavy overcast that began not too long after the noon hour. It had also become quite windy. The leaves flew by the windows of local offices and department stores in the main section of town.

Some of these leaves happened to fly by the window of a restaurant called Nick's, where Janet and Mike were having lunch across from hospital. Janet stared off into space for a bit, looking at the wondrous assortment of colors that went by outside, appreciating their beauty.

This was her favorite time of the year, for as long as she could remember she loved the brisk weather that accompanied autumn. Memories of her and her father raking up leaves in their backyard came to mind. Despite Margaret giving instructions on what to do with the leaves, she routinely had to break up Janet and Ted from throwing them at each other. Sometimes Margaret even got into it, and within minutes over an hour's work was ruined. Though they'd make a huge mess, the three of them had such a lovely time. Ted would reappear from under a mound of leaves, only to get more dumped on his head by his daughter and wife, and as retaliation he would grab both of them, pulling them to the ground. Once the trio became too tired they'd clean up the mess before dusk settled in and Ted would treat his favorite ladies out to a nice dinner. Janet's parents would take her out to Aunt Cecilia's and the three of them would share a large pepperoni and sausage pizza with extra cheese.

Janet sat there, her daydream so intense she could smell the aroma of each slice as she sat quietly, gazing out the restaurant window as the leaves flew by, totally unaware that Mike had been talking for some time.

"So you almost caused Bill to crash his phone, huh?" he said. "Would've served him right. He talks too much on that damn thing anyway."

Realizing Mike just asked her a question Janet re-directed her attention to the table.

"Yeah, I don't know what came over me," Janet replied. "I guess I'm still a bit jumpy because of these crazy nightmares I've been having."

Mike reached over to Janet, gently stroking her left hand, trying to reassure her as he did last night that everything was all right.

"Don't worry about those dreams, baby. You've got me here and I'm not going anywhere," Mike said, picking up her right hand and kissing it. "Did you talk to him about changing the dosage of your medication?"

She nodded. He recommended Cardizem for my high blood pressure. He feels it'll work with the Xanax."

She reached into her coat pocket and pulled out the prescription Bill gave her before she left, showing it to Mike. He cupped her hands in his and glanced at the prescription. Janet could see his eyes run across the paper, then gaze directly into hers. He held her right hand gingerly, again giving a feeling of reassurance that everything was fine.

Janet's eyes glistened as she looked at him with great affection, but her thoughts replayed their previous conversation from this morning. Remembering that Mike had lied about his whereabouts caused her to pull away from him, sitting further back into her chair. Her wide smile was now gone, replaced by a slight frown as if he were guilty of something and she knew it.

"Baby, where were you this morning? I called the office looking for you not too long after we spoke and Judy said you didn't have an appointment until ten-thirty. You left the house before nine."

Mike's head turned to the side, shaking it in disgust.

"Damn that Judy! I told her not to say anything other than I was in with a patient."

Janet tilted her head this time. "Come again?" she said, noticeably perplexed.

A bright smile returned to Mike's face as he reached for her hands, touching them tenderly as before.

"I've got something for you dear. I had to go pick it up this morning before going into the office," he said, reaching into his suit coat.

Mike pulled out a long, thin case and placed it on the table, sliding it towards his dumbfounded wife. The outside of the case had "Weissman and Sons" monogrammed in gold cursive print.

Janet picked up the heavy case, staring at it. She knew it was something expensive by the feel. Her hands appeared to be shaking.

"What's in it?" she asked.

"You'll have to open it and find out," Mike replied, elbows on the table and hands folded, resting under his chin.

He looked as if he were asking one of his patients a question, waiting with great forbearance for their answer. That was Mike's specialty, and he was far better at it than Janet, who seemed both anxious to know what she held in her hand, yet was too nervous to look.

She took a deep breath and began to open the box. Mike could see her eyes sparkle when she realized inside was an 18-karat gold Rolex wristwatch. Many times Janet looked at a Rolex for herself, but she refused to spend the extra money, thinking more of getting something for Mike or perhaps for David if he needed supplies for school.

Now after all this time she finally had one.

"Oh Mike, it's lovely! I don't know what to say!"

"How about saying 'I'll wear it in good health'?" the waitress remarked, stooping down behind Janet's left shoulder, admiring the watch. "And you'd better hurry before I take it from you!"

Both Mike and Janet turned and laughed at the waitress. Neither one realized she'd been standing there, getting a good look at the sparkling Rolex. Janet nodded in agreement with the astute summation.

"She's got a point," she said, turning her head back towards Mike. "I'll wear it in good health." Janet had obviously forgiven Mike for lying about his whereabouts.

"I'll drink to that!" he said, raising his glass of iced tea in the air.

Janet removed the Rolex, turning the face over.

"What's this?" she asked.

There was a brief flutter in Mike's eyes, then caught himself. "Oh yeah...there's an inscription on the bottom. Take a look."

Written in very fine print, the inscription said: "To J, with love, M."

Janet's face began to glow as she reached out once again to her husband.

"Thank you so much baby!"

As Janet continued to admire her gift, her cell phone rang. She rummaged through her purse looking for it, while Mike picked up the prescription from the table. Janet was on the phone with someone from her office and it appeared to be something serious. As her call continued for an additional minute, Mike laid the paper on the table; his focus rock-solid. Finally Janet ended her conversation.

"All right Pam, tell Mr. Jefferson I'm on my way," Janet said. She hung up the phone.

"Sweetie I have to get going. It seems Rich Jefferson has paid us a surprise visit and needs to see me immediately."

"Okay Hon, I've got a few patients coming in this afternoon as well, so I need to get back to work."

They both rose from the table. Mike looked at the check and handed the waitress a wad of money, then assisted Janet with her coat. She gathered her purse and the prescription, then paused – looking at the piece of paper in her hand.

"Mike, would you be a dear and take these to the pharmacy for me? I'm not sure how long this will take, and I may forget to do it later."

"No problem," he said, placing the papers in his pocket. "I'll bring it home tonight."

"Great, thank you," Janet replied. "Oh, and if you get home first, give Charlie a call and set a time for dinner on Friday. He dropped by this morning and invited us over."

"I'll call him when I get back to the office," Mike promised.

She kissed him goodbye, thanking him again for her lovely gift, then hurried through the front doors of the restaurant.

Mike walked slowly outside, watching her cross the street to the parking lot. The wind howled as leaves flew by, causing him to button his black trench coat, keeping it from flying open. He had a rather odd look on his face as he watched her disappear into the elevator. He stood as if he were in a trance, absorbed by some unknown dilemma. He stared at his shoes, almost like a child would who'd done something wrong.

Mike could hear the town bell ring, announcing the quarter hour. He checked the time: one forty-five in the afternoon.

"I'd better get a move on!" he thought, making his way across the street toward the medical center.

Chapter Seven: Memories

The remainder of Thursday proved to be relatively quiet. Up to this point Janet no longer saw nor heard anything strange as she had just one day prior. In fact, for the first time in quite a while she enjoyed uninterrupted sleep, which gave her more energy. Much to Mike's delight, she also regained her sexual appetite. That Friday morning, the two of them were wrapped in each other's arms in the heat of tremendous passion.

The morning interlude was pleasing to both of them. Mike was a very good lover, and while passion may taper off with time, the two of them had a level of energy that could match a man and a woman in their early twenties. Unlike a much younger couple, the years together and the increased level of intimacy that followed made moments like these even better. It certainly didn't hurt that Mike came to know Janet's body and where her spots were over time, and right now Janet wasn't complaining.

While encased in his arms Janet couldn't tell whether they were newlyweds or nearing middle age. With each gasp Janet could hear her breathing become deeper and slower, sounding as if she were in an enclosed room.

As their rhythm continued to flow, Janet felt as if she were holding her breath for several seconds, then exhaling. Several images flash before her eyes, ranging from happy to sad moments of her life. Her mind flew to a myriad of places: their wedding, the day her son David was born, the phone call she received from her father when her mom died a few years ago. For those fleeting moments Janet even reflected on her father's death. That hit her particularly hard, even more so than watching her mother die slowly because of cancer. All of Janet's long string of boyfriends failed to meet the standards set by her father; that is, until she met Mike in college. He was the only one her father approved of, and as far as Janet was concerned, that was good enough for her.

Janet could see Mike's face becoming tense, for he too was nearing a climax. She reached up, feeling his muscles bulge and beads of sweat roll down the side of him. Stars filled her eyes, followed by a radiant light. Eventually she lost sight of Mike.

***

When her vision cleared Janet saw herself as a ten year-old child running towards the screen door of her parents' house. As she neared the door she could feel a gentle breeze blow softly across her face, followed by a warmness that caused her cheeks to tingle.

The day proved to be bright and sunny, as it was the first day of summer, and school had just let out for the year. Janet was on her way outside to meet her friend Lisa Williams, who'd rung the front doorbell. She wore a white t-shirt, cut off blue jeans, white socks and her brand new pair of converse sneakers her father bought. As a child Janet was quite the tomboy and wore out sneakers rather quickly.

She let Lisa inside and they stood there giggling about all the fun they'd have this summer, now that school was out of the way. The pair continued their giddy laughter until Lisa pushed Janet out of the way and slammed the front door. The sound was loud enough to catch Margaret's attention in the kitchen.

"You girls knock off that racket out there!" she shouted from around the corner.

"I'm sorry ma'am," Lisa replied, looking down at the hard wood floor, "but there was some strange lady out there asking me about Janet."

"Where?" Margaret asked, walking hurriedly out of the kitchen towards both girls.

Janet followed as .Lisa grabbed Margaret and pulled her into the living room, where she stopped in front of the window and pointed.

"There she is, right there!"

The look on Margaret's face made a quick change from inquisitive to angry when she saw a woman dressed entirely in black, staring at them from across the street. Janet wasn't certain, but the stranger looked like the woman she saw in front of the bus a few years ago.

"Excuse me!" Margaret said sternly.

She left both girls in the living room and stormed outside, slamming the door behind her. Janet and Lisa continued to stand in front of the window as Margaret confronted the woman in black.

Both ladies were in each other's faces, jawing back and forth. Though they couldn't tell what was being said, the girls heard muffled portions of the nasty exchange. The women were very animated with their gestures, and the conversation appeared to rise to a heated level.

Margaret began pointing in the woman's face and in one quick move the woman slapped her with her right hand. Margaret covered her face and stepped back in shock. Before she could say anything the woman turned and ran away.

Margaret crossed the street and entered the house, still covering her cheek. The girls ran to meet her as she walked inside, again slamming the door. The left side of her face was red.

"Mommy, are you okay?" Janet asked.

"Yes I'm fine!"

"Who was that lady?" Lisa asked.

"Don't you two worry about that! Go upstairs and play!"

Both girls looked down at the floor. Margaret, realizing that she had hurt their feelings, bent down and took both their hands, Lisa with her left, and Janet with her right.

"I'm sorry Lisa, I didn't mean to yell," she said, now very calm.

Still holding both girls' hands she looked at Janet.

"I'm sorry pumpkin, please forgive me," Margaret said.

Margaret let go of Janet's hand and tenderly touched her cheek, then leaned forward and kissed her.

***

Janet felt a kiss on her forehead, redirecting her attention to her smiling husband.

Both lay in the afterglow of their lovemaking, feeling exhausted, yet exhilarated. Mike straddled her body, gently touching her face.

"Hey sweetie I thought I lost you there for a second," he said with a smile.

"Mmmmmm...no, I'm fine honey. I enjoyed that one. Wish I had time for another."

Mike had a surprised look on his face as if to say: "you've got to be kidding."

"Sweetie, I'm afraid that will have to wait for later. I'm not as young as I used to be, you know." Mike laughed at himself.

"From that performance? You coulda fooled me."

Mike kissed her neck, smiling wide.

"Are you trying to get another Rolex?"

Janet giggled, grabbing his left hand, pulling him closer.

"Why don't we just lay here for a while, fall asleep, then wake up and fuck again? Who needs a job, food or money when we can cum like that twice in one day?"

"I'd agree with you, but I like living in this house. Besides, if we keep going to work we can live in here long enough to fuck in every room. And this house has a *lot* of rooms."

Janet pretended to mull through Mike's suggestion, then came to a conclusion:

"Well, when you put it that way..."

She rolled over, facing him, kissing his nose.

"...I guess we should go to work after all."

"I'm glad you see things my way," Mike replied, as his nude, sweat covered body rose from the bed.

Taking a moment to stretch, Mike walked into the bathroom in need of a shower, while Janet sat up in bed, pulling the sheet over her chest. She thought of the woman in black,

40

wondering who she was and whatever became of her. After that incident, she never saw her again.

Janet rose from bed and walked into her closet, trying to decide which suit to wear to the office. After all, she had a very busy day ahead of her.

Chapter Eight: "Seeing the Light"

"Goddamn straight girl! I was the first person to sell over five thousand pocket calculators in one quarter at my old company. Them sum-bitches didn't know what to do with themselves!"

Charlie Richardson was explaining at the dinner table when he decided to go into business for himself. He took a lot of pride in everything he did, from his humble beginnings as a business owner to his many hobbies, one of which included gun collecting. Charlie and Mike were best friends and spent a lot of time going over Charlie's impressive gun and rifle collection in his basement. Mike used to go deer hunting with his father as a child, so he was experienced in handling guns and rifles. This definitely played a factor in Charlie and Mike's "male bonding," and they were referred to as "fric-and-frac" by their wives. Over the years they'd become quite close.

It was almost nine-o'clock and the four of them were just finishing Maria's lasagna, and like always during this portion of their visit, it was time for Charlie to tell one of his famous stories. He sat at the head of the table wagging his index finger at Janet, who was trying her best to look interested. It wasn't that Charlie was boring, but rather it was the same story she'd heard perhaps twenty or thirty times over the years. Usually this particular tale was told after Charlie finished dinner and was treating himself to a few glasses of scotch. Duggan's Dew with a splash of seltzer water and a pinch of Marbella tobacco for his pipe and Charlie was in full storytelling mode.

Janet smiled because she knew what Charlie was going to say next. He was at the point where he was re-telling how his company was cheating him on his commissions and when he knew it was time to go into business for himself.

"...and that's when I saw the goddamn light," she thought, knowing that was coming out his mouth at any moment.

"You know what, girl...that's when I saw the goddamn light!"

Janet snickered. Mike, who was sitting across the table, nudged her leg with his left foot. Janet quickly straightened up and put her "truly interested" face back on. Maria Richardson rose from her seat, reaching over her verbose husband to collect his dishes.

"Charlie don't you ever get tired of telling that story?" she said, loading up her hands with silverware and plates. "We're going to lose Mike and Janet as friends if you keep boring them to death!"

"Aw hell, they don't mind at all! Surely you guys like that story, don't you?" Charlie asked.

"Uh...no...no, I never get tired of hearing it," Janet said.

She flashed a look at Mike, who knew she was lying through her teeth. Janet respected Charlie and would never do anything to hurt his feelings. Actually she not only found his stories quite inspiring, but also noted how passionate Charlie was when he would tell them. She knew he was proud of all that he'd achieved in his life. Janet appreciated hard work, a virtue she had learned from her father.

"Excuse me a sec, guys, I'll be right back," Mike said.

He stood, walked around the table and kissed his wife, then headed towards the bathroom. Maria walked back into the room to collect the remaining dishes and started with Janet's plate.

"I'll give you a hand with the dishes Maria," she said, standing up from the table.

"That's right girl! Bust some suds and earn yer keep, dammit!" Charlie chuckled, pounding his huge fist on the table.

Janet kissed Charlie on top of his head as she began assisting Maria, who wrapped her arms around her crass, yet tender, husband.

"If anyone needs to earn their keep around here, it's you!" Maria quipped.

"Shit woman, I'll earn my keep when they leave."

Charlie pinched his wife's backside, to which she giggled and playfully swatted his hand away before joining Janet in the kitchen.

***

Born into a poor family in the small town of Dushore, Pennsylvania, Charlie was the oldest of five children, four boys and one girl. No strangers to hard work, he and his siblings worked on the family farm until his father, Raymond Richardson, died in a horrible accident. His dad was a heavy drinker, and was known by the family to have a bottle of whiskey nearby while he was working.

One late August afternoon in 1945 Ray was operating a tractor when he lost his balance and fell over the left side, only to be crushed by the tractor's rear wheels. Seventeen-year-old Charlie happened to be nearby and heard his father screaming, eventually finding his dad face down in the ground. The tractor had run Ray over and continued moving down the field. Charlie sprinted after the tractor and shut it off, then returned to his father's side. He was barely alive, and when Charlie turned him over he was gagging on his own blood. His chest and arms were crushed. Charlie began crying, trying to comfort Ray, stroking his face.

"I'm sorry, son!" Ray gurgled, spitting up blood. "So sorry...sorry...."

"Relax dad, I'll go get some help."

Charlie tried to stand, but Ray grabbed him with his left hand, screaming because of the intense pain. He looked into Charlie's eyes.

"Don't...be like your old man...a drunk," he said, still coughing up blood. "Sell this place...move away. Keep the...family together."

"Dad, don't say such things," Charlie said, tearfully. "Just relax, you'll be all right."

"I love you...tell them...that I love ..."

Ray looked directly into Charlie's eyes, his left hand reaching for his face. Before he could touch his son, Ray's hand slumped to the ground, and he closed his eyes forever.

Not long afterward Charlie did what his father requested. He and Joan, his mother, sold the farm and used the proceeds to purchase a home for her in Williamsport, where she resided until she passed away five years later. He made arrangements for her to be buried next to his father in Dushore and assumed the role as head of the family.

Charlie kept everyone together by going to work for the novelty company in State College, and through his sacrificing he put all of his siblings through Penn State, though he himself did not go to college. One brother, Roger, lived in Philadelphia until he died of a heart attack in 1983, Ray Jr. lives in Fort Lauderdale, Peter moved to Long Island, NY where he lives with his family, and Linda resides in San Diego. Though there is a great deal of distance between them, they all stay in touch with one another and get together as a family each Christmas and New Year's.

Charlie made good on his father's wishes.

***

He stood and walked over to the liquor cabinet reaching again for *the Dew*, as he often called it. He poured himself a glass and walked out to the front porch. Pipe firmly planted in his teeth, he took a couple of puffs then exhaled, closing his eyes briefly as he felt the cool air rush across his face, taking in the serenity of the moment. It was quiet outside with only the occasional sound of a passing car to interrupt the peace. Charlie opened his eyes and sat down on the steps of his porch.

If someone were looking at him from a distance in the darkness, they could see his pipe glow brightly each time he took a puff.

45

Chapter Nine: Love at First Sight

    Charlie continued to puff away in the night air, his thoughts careening through a series of vignettes from special moments in his life. Steady bursts of smoke rose from his lips and nose as he unconsciously grinned to himself, pleased at the scenes that played out before him. The sixties were difficult times for the Richardson Family, but Charlie wasn't focused on that right now. Instead, he thought of Maria - when they met, the special moments they've shared together and how his life has been blessed ever since.

***

July 17, 1965

    After his mother's passing, Charlie took a job at The Nittany Novelty Company in State College as a door-to-door salesman. The job paid $.75 an hour, which was good for the1960s, but the real money came from quarterly bonuses and commissions. Besides the money Charlie amassed from the sales of the farm in Dushore and the Williamsport home, he made enough to take care of his other siblings. He was tough, but also very much a nurturing father figure to each of them, taking the burden left behind by the death of both parents. Charlie worked long hours, sometimes six days a week, to ensure that he had enough to pay their tuition, for they would be the first to graduate college in his family.

Charlie didn't have time for a social life, let alone a steady girlfriend. He hardly knew anyone outside of work and the few church friends he got together with on occasion. If he wasn't working he was busy fixing things at the home he'd purchased for the family. Sometimes one of his siblings would have friends over, so he would assist in the kitchen and help decorate, all the while sacrificing his own needs for them.

One Tuesday afternoon during the Summer of '65 Charlie was busy knocking on doors in nearby Lemont when he came to a white house on Pike Street. The house and grounds were surrounded by a white picket fence, and the backyard had an old stone well located next to a large oak tree. There were freshly planted flowers along both sides of the house and the grass appeared to have been recently cut. Charlie took a few moments admiring the work that had been put into the house and wondered what it had sold for. Most of the homes in Lemont resembled this one in terms of upkeep, as the folks that lived there were fairly affluent. Lemont was a small town of about a thousand people, but then again nothing was really small being so close to State College. The Penn State community had a strong hold throughout all of Howard County, and whether or not people actually attended the University, the Nittany Lion could be seen on nearly every door, front lawn or picket fence, and since Charlie had siblings who were current students, the Richardson household was no exception.

Charlie opened the gate and walked towards the front door, suitcase in hand. He was dressed in a gray suit, one of three that he owned, and a matching fedora rested on his head. Even though it was the middle of July he still understood the importance of making a proper first impression. It was an attitude like this that enabled him to make "Salesman of the Month" for nine months running.

He knocked on the door and stepped back, taking in the neighborhood while waiting for someone to answer the door. Directly across the street a teenager was mowing their lawn.

There were kids that appeared to be playing jacks on the sidewalk, the shade from a large tree keeping them cool.

Further down the block he could see an elderly couple sitting on the front stoop, rocking gently back and forth in their chairs with a small table in between them with two glasses sitting on it. They appeared to be sleeping, but they were holding hands. No doubt they've been together for many years, something that Charlie had hoped for as he got older. He could see it now, his kids bringing the grandchildren over for dinner on Sunday evenings, everyone gathered around a large dinner table in the dining room covered with meat, potato and vegetable dishes with freshly baked bread and sweet potato pie for dessert. Charlie would play the grandpa role, bouncing the kids on his knee and telling whopper stories of what life was like when he was young. The only thing missing from this entire vision was a wife – something that he'd not made time to look for because time wasn't something that was available to him at the moment.

"Yes can I help you?" a woman's voice said behind him.

Charlie turned to introduce himself, business card in hand, when he froze in his tracks. He was looking into the eyes of the most beautiful woman he'd ever seen, and for once in his life had no idea what to say. She had long brown hair; hazel colored eyes and a lovely smile that spoke to Charlie in ways he's never known before. She wore a blue polka dot dress and had a lovely heart shaped silver pendant around her neck. The sweet scent of her perfume had Charlie mesmerized.

The woman looked at this speechless salesman in a puzzled fashion, tilting her head to the right, then asked the question a second time.

"Can I help you?" she asked again. Her smile widened as she waited patiently for his response. Charlie took a deep breath and introduced himself.

"I'm Charles Richardson and I work for the Nittany Novelty Company. I was wondering if you had a few moments to take a look at some of our new gift ideas."

Charlie fumbled around looking for the lock on his briefcase, never taking his eyes off of the woman in the blue dress. As he opened it, the contents of his briefcase spilled onto her front porch, causing the woman to laugh, while Charlie began to turn red from embarrassment. He quickly knelt to straighten the mess he'd made.

"Here, let me help you with that," she said, bending over gathering his things.

"Real nice, huh?" Charlie said, chuckling to himself. "I feel like a rookie on his first day. How clumsy of me."

"Oh not to worry, I don't mind. In fact, I'm glad you're here. I could use a few things for a friends' birthday that's coming up soon. Why don't you come in and show me what you have?"

"Swell. By the way, I'm Charles Richardson," Charlie said, extending his hand. He felt silly; realizing he'd already said his name once.

"My name is Maria Riley," she replied, shaking his hand. "I just moved here from Wilkes-Barre and I'll be teaching English at the university this fall."

Charlie was amazed. From listening to his siblings discuss the classes they were taking this semester, he didn't' think there were any female professors at the university.

She invited him inside and he went through his presentation in her living room. Charlie ended up selling $20 worth of items, nearly half of what he had in his briefcase for the week. Maria went on to say that some of these items were for friends who had birthdays coming up soon, while the others she would give away as Christmas gifts. That coupled with the $35 in sales he'd already received made for a very successful day, one in which he decided to spend the remainder of the day talking to her.

Charlie spent the next three hours telling her about his family, his parents who were now deceased and what it was like being a top salesman for a small novelty company. He also revealed that eventually one day he wanted a business of his own. Maria sat there smiling at him the entire time, hardly speaking much. Here and there she offered bits of her past – her parents having passed away as well, her being an only child and wanting to teach on the college level, which was not

49

commonplace for women of her time. She kept her comments brief so she could hear more about Charlie, seemingly enthralled by his passion and zest for life. Unbeknownst to her at the time, this feeling would remain strong throughout their life together.

Charlie checked his watch, realizing it was getting late. He hurriedly stood from her couch, grabbing his briefcase.

"I'm sorry, but I need to go. I have to get home so I can handle dinner for the family."

"Well thank you Charlie for coming by. You've made my gift shopping a lot easier this year, thank you."

"Not a problem Maria, please refer me to your friends if they have similar needs."

He handed her a few business cards.

She promised to do so, escorting him to the front door. After another goodbye, Charlie turned and walked out the front gate, closing it behind him as Maria watched him stroll down the block.

It was a pleasant evening, so she left her screen door open, allowing a gentle breeze to flow gently through her living room. Maria continued to smile as she went to prepare a meal for herself in the kitchen, when her telephone rang a few moments later. The caller was Charlie, and he stopped at a pay phone at a gas station about a block away.

"Hi Maria, it's Charlie. Listen I'm not good at this sort of thing, but I wanted to know if you'd like to..."

"Yes, I'd love to!" she interrupted. "How about Saturday at seven-thirty?"

"Umm...uh...sure, Saturday is fine!" Charlie stammered. He hadn't expected this type of response, but was relieved that she said yes.

And it was nearly a year where she would say "yes" to him again; this time it was to a proposal of marriage. Never in a million years had Charlie expected someone as lovely as her to get married to a crazy bum like him. Four children, nine grandchildren, a family business and forty-three years later he still wondered the same thing.

Chapter Ten: A Night to Confess

"Enjoying the night air?" he heard a voice from behind him say.

It was Mike, and he took a seat on the steps next to Charlie.

"Somewhat," Charlie replied. "I'm just trying to relax a bit. It's been a rough day for me."

Mike agreed and started to say something when Charlie interrupted him.

"I have to tell you something Mike, but you have to keep this to yourself, ok?"
Charlie's usual gruff demeanor had changed to a more reserved one. Mike turned his body toward his friend, giving him his full attention.

"Of course Charlie, you know me," Mike replied.

"I...I cheated on Maria," he mumbled, not being able to look Mike in the eye.

Mike touched Charlie's shoulder, immediately feeling the tension in his body. Charlie was trembling, and it was obvious he was very remorseful for what he'd done.

"Have you told Maria about it?"

"No I haven't, and I'm debating if I should or shouldn't. This happened a few weeks ago with someone I met while on a business trip to Pittsburgh. I went out for a couple of drinks after some meetings with my distributors. I met this beautiful young woman as I was about to leave. She and I kept drinking and talking...and the next thing I know..."

Charlie's head fell into his hands. He was trembling even more now and Mike could hear him sobbing. Mike patted his back. In all the years he'd known Charlie, Mike had never seen him like this before. Charlie tried to calm himself but failed miserably.

"I don't know what I'm going to do. I'm not sure if I should tell my wife or not," Charlie said, turning and finally looking Mike in the eye.

"What do you think I should do?"

Mike sat quietly for a moment.

"Does this woman know where you live or how to get in touch with you?" Mike asked.

"No," Charlie replied, shaking his head. "Hell man, I don't think she knows my last name. When it became obvious that things were progressing I said very little."

"Well – if I were you I'd keep this between us. I see no reason for bringing it up, especially after all the years you two have shared together. Just leave it alone. You made a mistake, so move on. I won't say anything if you won't, okay?"

Mike extended his hand, making a pact with Charlie to keep his word.

Charlie sat motionless for a moment, pondering Mike's suggestion when a smile crept back on his face. He shook Mike's hand.

"You're right. The last thing I wanna do is hurt Maria with this after all our years together. Thanks buddy, I'm really lucky to have a friend like you."

"Hey brother, what are friends for?" Mike said, slapping Charlie on the back.

The two friends sat next to one another, enjoying the serenity of the evening for several minutes. Charlie continued puffing away at his pipe when Mike finally broke the silence.

"Charlie, may I ask a personal question?"

"Sure, what's up?"

Mike looked directly at his friend; a wicked smile covered his face.

"So how was it?" he asked.

At first Charlie didn't know what Mike was referring to, then an embarrassed look slowly crept across his face.

"Well...to be honest, I don't remember much of anything. We went back to my room and started making out. The next thing I knew, it was morning and I was in bed. Alone."

Mike began to laugh, further relieving Charlie of his guilt. Their laughter continued until Janet rushed out the front door wearing her sweater, ready to leave. Something was wrong; she looked as if she'd just seen a ghost.

"Honey, I'm not feeling well," she said, "do you mind if we go now?"

"Is there somethin' wrong?" Charlie asked, a slight grin appearing on his face. "You get attacked by a giant soap bubble?"

Janet mustered a smile, but found it difficult to look him in the eye.

"No, no silly – I just have a headache. I must've overdone it with the Seagram's Seven."

Charlie chuckled at her response, flashing a wicked grin at Mike.

"I guess someone ain't getting any tonight," he whispered in Mike's ear.

Mike stifled a snicker as Maria came outside with a glass of water and some ibuprofen, handing it to Janet. She also had Mike's jacket over her shoulder and after giving Janet her tablets she gave the jacket to Mike.

"Here you go dear," Maria said. "Take this – you'll feel much better after you get a good night's rest."

"Thanks Maria. I'm sorry if I appear in a rush to leave but I just want to go home and lie down."

"Not a problem dear," Maria replied, taking the glass from Janet. "Go home, get some rest. I'll give you a call in the morning."

After exchanging goodbyes Mike and Janet walked home, not speaking from the time they entered the house until they began getting ready for bed.

Mike curled up next to her, noticing Janet remained distant. He appeared to be concerned and touched his wife on the shoulder, causing her to jump.

"What's wrong, sweetie?" he asked. "Still not feeling well?"

Janet looked at him and, taking a deep breath, began to speak.

"Well...it's probably nothing, but I just can't help feeling this way," she began.

Janet took another deep breath.

"You remember me telling you I got that weird note along with the book?"

"Yes," Mike replied, holding her hand.

"Well...I went to the bathroom after helping Maria with the dishes. Charlie left a magazine on the sink, so I started looking through it when I noticed several pages with missing letters. It just made me think if he was the one who sent that note. I know he said he didn't, but I can't help but wonder."

Mike chuckled. "Well that sure sounds like something he'd do, and I wouldn't doubt it. You know Charlie – he's notorious for pulling cheap pranks. Don't let it get to you, sweetie. After what he and I discussed this evening, I doubt if he was involved. But even if he was, you and I both know Charlie has a habit of taking a joke too far. If he did anything I doubt the intent was malicious."

"What did he have to say to you?" she asked, turning over and facing him directly.

Mike chose his words carefully.

"Not much," he replied. "Just a bunch of work related issues he concerned about, nothing more."

Mike leaned over and kissed her. Gently caressing her cheek, he looked into her eyes.

"Don't worry about it, all right? I'm here, and I promise nothing is going to happen to you," he said, kissing her again. "Let's get some rest."

Mike shut off the light and turned to his right side, holding Janet around her waist. While she quickly fell asleep, Mike was still thinking about Charlie's confession of "alleged" infidelity. He kept running that conversation through his mind over and over again, hearing Charlie's response: *"We went back to my room and started making out. The next thing I knew, it was morning and I was in bed. Alone."*

Those words rang in his head for nearly an hour, until he finally fell asleep.

Chapter Eleven: Betrayal

Thump, thump! Thump, thump!

"No!" Janet screamed, sitting up from her leather couch. She'd been dreaming again, her nightgown covered in sweat.

It was a Saturday morning. The mood outside was dark and gloomy as the rain came down in buckets, leaving huge puddles everywhere. Janet reached for her near empty bottles of Cardizem and Xanax sitting on her coffee table, popped pills into her mouth and chased them down with a leftover glass of Jack and Coke from the previous evening.

She grabbed her remote control and turned on the television. The morning news was on and was surprised to see the anchorman wearing a Count Dracula outfit, while their sports reporter was sitting next to him wearing a Philadelphia Phillies baseball uniform with Len Dykstra's number.

"Happy Halloween," Janet whispered. She checked the time. 7:17 am.

Earlier that week Mike went to visit his sister in Cleveland and wouldn't be back until tomorrow morning, giving her needed time to focus on the Jefferson trial that ended in victory yesterday. It was a long and tiring process, but the result was as she expected, and yesterday she had a private celebration at home. Mike promised to treat her out to a nice evening when he returned.

Janet hated sleeping alone and would always turn her couch into a makeshift bed, covering it with sheets and a warm quilt, as well as bed pillows when Mike was out of town. She even brought something down to read in case of insomnia, which was almost every night this week. Janet's nightmares continued infrequently throughout the month, and though she believed the new prescriptions were making progress, she still found herself occasionally waking up on edge.

She took a second glance at her sweat-ridden nightgown and decided to head upstairs and take a shower, after which she draped herself in a soft white cashmere robe and slippers, then began to dry her hair. The storm was so heavy outside that she could hear it coming down with the dryer running, and took a second to look out the bathroom window.

Finding it hard to see anything, she continued on with her hair until it was dry, then headed down to the kitchen, pouring herself a glass of cranberry juice. The wind shrieked as she watched the trees outside sway back and forth. Except for the lightning, it was almost as dark as night outside, and the thunder cracked so loudly it shook the house. She hoped by the time Mike began his trip home the rain would have moved on.

"I wonder if the weather is as bad in Ohio," she thought.

Janet took one last sip of juice, then placed her glass on the counter and headed towards the phone when she heard a humming noise coming from behind her. The sound came from the dumbwaiter. It was coming up from the basement.

She walked slowly toward it, looking carefully into the darkness until it stopped in front of her. The thunder roared. What sat in front of her was a jack-o-lantern and an envelope, the name "Janet" in cut out letters on the front.

She opened the envelope and pulled out a piece of paper that read: *London Bridge is Falling Down, My Fair Lady*.

"What the..."

A brick crashed through the window, hit the refrigerator and landed on the floor.

Thump, thump! Thump, thump!

Janet screamed and ran out of the kitchen, heading for the staircase. Mike's 9mm was in the upstairs closet.

Thump, thump! Thump, thump!

She reached the top of the stairs, gasping heavily for air. The dumbwaiter hummed; it was coming up again, this time at the other end of the upstairs hallway.

Janet stood there, clutching her heart, completely frozen by fear of what might be there, when it finally came to a full stop. She couldn't see anything except for darkness. Each second lasted a lifetime. She tried the light switch. It didn't work. The gloomy weather outside made it hard to make out anything, so cautiously she made her way toward the dumbwaiter.

Suddenly thunder struck, the lightning brightened up the hallway. There was a large man dressed in black standing in front of her. He had a serrated knife in his right hand, blood running down his face. Janet stood face to face with the figure in her dreams, and he began to walk very slowly and calmly towards her, the knife giving off the brightest light in the hallway.

For every step backward, *He* took one toward her. The man closed in as she headed for the stairs, desperately gasping for air. She grabbed her chest and fell against the banister.

Thump, thump! Thump, thump!

Before the man in black could attack her, Janet collapsed and fell down the staircase, striking her head violently against the wall, blood splattered everywhere. Once her body came to a complete stop the figure walked down and bent over her. Removing the glove from his right hand he tested for a pulse. She was gone.

The man in black removed his mask, a horrified look covered his face. It was Charlie, and as he continued to stare at Janet's motionless body the reality of what just happened began to sink in further. He began to tremble.

"Oh God...oh my God, what have I done?" he sobbed.

Charlie fell backwards against the staircase then scrambled to his feet, rubbing his hands and arms. Tears were streaming down his face and he began crying like a wounded animal that had just broken its leg. His mind was racing wildly, wondering what he was going to do and how he could explain this to the police.

There was no way around it. He knew this was a scandal waiting to happen and his life would be ruined because of it. All that he'd worked for would be reduced to ashes; his wife, children, family would all leave him and he'd be in jail for the rest of his life. Here he was, breaking into his next-door neighbor's house, wearing dark clothing with a mask and a knife.

Charlie's life, as he knew it, was finished. That's all he could think about now.

"Oh sweet Jesus! Janet, I'm so sorry!" he sobbed, kneeling down next to her, gently touching her right hand. "I really didn't mean to..."

The sound of footsteps approached him from the darkness. He looked up and saw Mike walking very calmly toward him, his hands firmly planted inside the pockets of his rain soaked trench coat.

Saying nothing to Charlie he pulled out a pack of Marlboro Red cigarettes. He lit a cigarette with a silver flip-top liter, the "clink" sound registered as he snapped it shut. Mike didn't smoke often, and never smoked around Janet, but for obvious reasons he felt okay in doing it now. After taking a drag and blowing a huge cloud of smoke into the air he focused his attention on what was before him.

"What seems to be the problem Charlie?" he hissed.

Mike took another drag from the cigarette. Only his silhouette appeared to Charlie in the darkness, with the occasional lightning revealing Mike's true self. Charlie looked into his eyes; they were hollow, cold - like the weather outside. This look caused Charlie to tremble more violently. In his mind he was looking directly into the eyes of the devil.

"What the fuck does it look like?" "Your wife is fucking dead! This wasn't supposed to happen like this! We were only playing a joke on her!"

"What do you mean, wasn't supposed to happen?" Mike snapped. "This is how we worked it out. You were supposed to break in and scare her.

Putting on a grin that looked every bit like Dr. Martin's, he said: "From the look of things I'd say you did just that."

He took one last drag, walked over to the living room table, grabbed a coaster and put the cigarette out. Placing his hands back in his pockets again he walked back towards Charlie, then continued:

"The only problem is you killed her in the process. I want to thank you, Charlie. You've done me a tremendous favor."

"You...you *planned* this?" Charlie said, trying to stand up straight. "The letters, the book...all of this? You set me up?"

He took a step toward Mike, who drew a gun on him. Charlie stopped in his tracks. The barrel was pointed in his face. He didn't dare move, for he felt certain Mike would shoot him if he did. Instead he stood perfectly still, holding both hands up where Mike could see them.

"Yeah, and you came along for the ride. Now sit your ass down!" Mike snapped.

He motioned Charlie over to the living room couch, where a pen and notepad sat on the table.

Charlie sat down quietly. He'd stopped sobbing, but the trembling continued. He again looked at Mike, who sat on a love seat adjacent to the couch; he was still pointing the gun at him. Charlie still could only see Mike's silhouette sitting next to him. The thunder continued rumbling outside.

"You'll never get away with this Mike," Charlie said. "Someone will find out, and they'll..."

"They'll what? They'll think it was me? I don't think so Charlie. After you're dead the police will find those letters you gave Janet in the bottom drawer of the desk in your office, along with a neatly packaged envelope containing pictures of you and your mistress and a typed letter from Janet demanding money. You see, Janet was blackmailing you, but instead of paying you decided to kill her instead. You sent her those letters; you broke in here and attacked her. She falls down the stairs and cracks open her fucking skull. You suddenly realized what you did and felt tremendous remorse, so you wrote a suicide letter and took your own life. I came in from my sister's place in Ohio wanting to surprise my wife a day early and found both your bodies lying

60

here on the floor. Oh yes mon ami, they most certainly will think it was you...oh, and by the way, I hope you don't mind me using your own gun to shoot you. I can't have this traced back to me, now can I? You really shouldn't show your friends where you keep your gun collections you know. It isn't safe."

Charlie was totally helpless, realizing that he was about to die. Mike told him to pick up the pen and instructed him to write the following: *I'm so sorry. I didn't mean it. May God forgive me, Charlie.*

After he finished writing, Charlie dropped the note, and while Mike bent over to pick it up Charlie quickly reached out and grabbed the gun.

The two men began struggling in the living room. They wrestled each other to the floor, knocking over a picture, a few coasters, including the one with the cigarette ashes, and some magazines that were on the living room table. Though Mike was a strong man Charlie wrested the gun away from him, cocked the gun and pointed it Mike, who was still lying on the floor with his hands in front of him. Despite the fact he'd been disarmed; Mike was very cool and lay there smiling.

"What are you going to do Charlie, shoot me?" Mike said, a huge smirk on his face. "Either way you're going to be blamed for this. Not only did you kill Janet, but you murdered me too! You'll get The Chamber for this and you know it."

Charlie began to realize the devil was right. He stood there mulling through a multitude of scenarios, but to no avail. There was nothing pointing directly to Mike as the culprit for Janet's murder. Instead all the signs were against him. One way or another he was a dead man and he knew it. With this in mind, there was only one thing left to do. He stopped shaking, laughing like a madman.

"Then I'll see you in hell!" Charlie screamed.

He placed it next to his head, pulling the trigger. A loud bang and it was all over; his body slumped along the side of the couch, making a loud *thud* as he crashed to the floor. The floor was smeared with blood and his legs were flailing about in a spasm.

Finally he stopped kicking, his body became perfectly still.

Mike stood up and looked at Charlie's corpse, then turned and faced Janet.

"Finally it's over," he whispered to himself.

Mike reached into his pocket and held two zip-loc bags, one filled with large green capsules, the other with white tablets. Stepping carefully over the blood so he wouldn't get anything on his shoes he walked around the house searching for Janet's prescriptions, finding them in the den next to the empty glass she'd left on the table.

After locating Janet's near-empty bottles, Mike went to the kitchen sink and poured the contents into the garbage disposal, filling up the bottle with the real medication that Dr. Martin originally prescribed. Mike had taken a supply of placebo that he used in a study he performed ten months earlier and replaced her prescriptions with those. Janet was given something completely useless in helping her condition, which had worsened from nightmares and work related stress. She was left vulnerable to a heart attack. Mike knew with good planning and patience, this would be possible to pull off.

"It worked like a charm," he thought.

Since he had some of Charlie's blood on his trench coat he grabbed a hefty bag from under the kitchen sink and went upstairs to his bedroom to change into fresh clothing. Mike took the coat and placed it into the bag, then returned to the top of the staircase, looking down at the dead bodies before him. He noticed the items he knocked over from the living room table and went down to examine them. Miraculously none of Charlie's blood was on any of the items, so he neatly placed them back on the table like they once were. He also took the cigarette-smeared coaster and put it in a bag, as well as the jack-o-lantern and the note from the kitchen.

He strode out the side door in the den, carrying the bag over his shoulder in the rain through his backyard. Instead of parking his car in front of the house, Mike left it a block away. It sat behind a large tree on a relatively empty side street.

Keeping an eye out for anyone who might see him he placed the bag in the trunk and drove until he found a dumpster, then stopped the car and threw the hefty bag inside. Returning home and parking in the driveway he walked through the front door with an overnight bag on his shoulder. He took a moment to look around the room, making a final sweep of the area. Once he was satisfied he reached for the phone and dialed 911. The time was now nine forty-five in the morning.

It was true perfidy in motion!

"My wife...she's dead, she's dead," he said, sobbing over the phone.

Within fifteen minutes an ambulance and a police car pulled up in front of the house. While the paramedics were taking care of the bodies, the police asked Mike a series of questions.

Mike told them that Janet's cardiologist had prescribed her Cardizem and Xanax for her heart condition, but often she forgot to take her medication or refused to do so altogether, saying she didn't need it. He also mentioned he decided to surprise her by coming home a day early from his trip to Ohio, only to find her and Charlie lying in the living room and the suicide note just a few feet from Charlie's dead body.

After a few more questions the officers expressed their condolences to Mike and promised to investigate this matter further, starting with Charlie's house. Lord knows what was in store for Maria once she discovered what happened.

The police left, as did the paramedics, for they'd already loaded both corpses into the ambulance. Mike had given the officers all the information they needed in case they wanted him to come in for questioning. He shut the door and picked up the telephone in the living room. The first call was to his son at school, who naturally was quite upset to hear the news. He then dialed another number on a pre-paid cell phone.

"Yes I'm all right, he said to the listener. "We'll have to be careful a while, but it'll all work if we stick to the plan."

Mike spoke on the phone for a few more minutes, then hung up and walked upstairs, a tremendous weight being lifted

63

from his shoulders. He took a shower, crashed on the couch in the den – the same place where Janet slept this past week.

After a few minutes of twisting and turning, he fell into a deep sleep - completely unaware that a mysterious stranger dressed in a trench coat was standing in the rain across the street from the house holding a light blue umbrella.   As the figure continued to observe the house, the town hall announced it was eleven o'clock, prompting the stranger to turn away and walk slowly down the block.

Chapter Twelve: Morningside

Mike stood by the front gates of Morningside Cemetery dressed in a black suit and shoes, white shirt and black tie. A bouquet of white roses in his right hand, he gazed down the curved road of the entrance, placed his hands around the bars and scanned the area, noting the beautifully landscaped grounds, rolling hills, large trees and the array of tombstones from simple designs to very elaborate and finely sculptured monuments. The road eventually led to a mausoleum in the center of the cemetery's forty acres. By far it was the largest of the three cemeteries in Erie County. The entrance featured a circular path with a water fountain in the center. The fountain had an eleven-foot sculpture of Saint Callistus, who wore a long, flowing robe. His left hand held a book, the right was raised high in the air; the artist's portrayal of him appeared as if he were in the middle of a blessing.

Saint Callistus was born into slavery, owned by Carpophorus who was in the house of Caesar. Supposedly Carpophorus trusted Callistus with funds to open a bank, but when people failed to repay their loans Callistus knew he would be blamed. Forced to flee for his life, he eventually was caught and sentenced to work in the tin mines. After later being bailed out of his sentence by other Christians he eventually was put in charge of the public burial grounds of Rome by Pope Saint Zephryinus. In memoriam, today those burial grounds are called the Cemetery of Saint Callistus. Mike was well aware of the life of Callistus, being that he and his sister Rebecca grew up in a Catholic household were they were taught the various patron saints.

"Good ole BC," he thought. 'BC' meaning 'Baltimore Catechism', which was the traditional mode of study in Catholic schools until 1964. Now it's referred to as the Catechism of the Catholic Church, and those studying to become Catholic are called Catechumens.

The gates in front of the cemetery had opened and a series of limousines and cars came rolling by. It appeared a burial had just taken place and the procession was leading back towards the center of town. Mike watched as the last car went by, and then walked past the fountain, heading down the long, winding road. As he walked deeper into the cemetery he noticed the sky suddenly became cloudy, covering the sun as if it were about to rain. The trees swayed from the wind. Mike folded his arms together, rubbing his shoulders to keep warm, when suddenly he heard a voice call his name.

"Michael..............Michael".....

Mike stopped in the middle of the road and looked around. He saw no one.

"Where are you?" he asked.

"Over here Michael.........I'm waiting for you."

Mike turned around. Off in the distance was an open grave, probably the same one the mourners that left the cemetery were visiting.

"That's it Michael.........come to me. Come to me, Michael," the Voice hissed.

Mike saw a figure standing in front of the grave with their back turned to him. Dressed in a long black robe with a hood and holding a wooden staff in their left hand, the person appeared to be an old woman. Mike could see a black onyx on her left index finger. Her fingernails were painted black and matted strands of gray hair came from under her hood. The woman trembled, and the closer Mike came he clearly heard her sobs.

She turned around facing Mike, her hood covering most of her face. She was quite old, well into her eighties; heavy wrinkles, scraggly hairs and age spots dotted her chin. Her mouth gnarled up, angered by Mike's presence. She pointed her long staff directly in his face.

"What are you doing here? You killed her! You are responsible for her death!" she screamed.

Mike began to back away from her. "I....I didn't kill anyone old woman! I have no idea what you're talking about!"

He backed into a tree. The old woman came closer to him, staff still pointing at him.

"Don't lie. You killed her and you must pay!" she screamed.

The old woman grabbed Mike around the neck and lifted him into the air. With one hand she carried him to the open grave, dangling him over it as Mike struggled. The wind picked up. Leaves blew against his face. Thunder rumbled. His eyes begged for mercy, but the old woman merely appeared fascinated by his terrified expression.

Thump, thump! Thump, thump!

She gave him a menacing smile and dropped him into the grave. Mike's head struck the casket, dazing him momentarily until he was aroused by something being dropped on him. The old woman began shoveling dirt on top of him. She was burying him alive. A hand punched through the casket and grabbed him by the forehead, pulling him tightly against it. Mike gagged violently; the dirt piled on top of his face until he could no longer see...

***

Mike thrashed about in bed; Jasmine held onto him until he finally calmed down.

"I'm alright, babe. It was just another nightmare."

"Are you sure you're okay?" Jasmine asked.

"I'm fine," he reassured her, "I just need to get back to sleep."

Mike tenderly kissed his wife of nearly two years and turned over, acting as if he were going back to sleep. Instead he stared out into the storm; a lightning flash momentarily brightened their room. Over the crackle of thunder, Mike heard the grandfather clock strike midnight from the hallway, one of the few possessions from his former life that he actually kept.

Mike found it difficult to get back to sleep, and after nearly two hours of tossing and turning, he finally nodded off, though it proved to be a fitful rest. It was the fear of the unknown that had haunted him for several nights in a row.

Indeed he had a right to be afraid. This coming Halloween, which was just a few short days away, would make it three years since Janet's tragic death.

Mike hated this time a year with a passion.

***

During the summer of 1998 Mike was in Chicago for a week-long conference at the Drake Hotel. During his down time he took a stroll into Marshall Fields in the Water Tower Place on Michigan Avenue to do some shopping, and it was as he was looking at shoes in the men's section when he first saw Jasmine. She was young, beautiful and successful in her own right. She worked as a fashion buyer for Field's and was in the middle of touring the store with a group of summer interns when they first met.

"Excuse me, Miss...Kaye," he said, reading her nametag.

"Yes, how can I help you?" she asked. Her hazel eyes seemed to sparkle as Mike approached her.

"I was wondering if you had a pair of these black loafers in my size."

They smiled tenderly at one another. Finally Jasmine broke away and examined the brown Clark's slip-ons that were currently on his feet.

"Size eleven, regular...right?"

Mike was impressed. "Perfect."

Jasmine sent a male intern to find a sales clerk and sat there until Mike found exactly what he was looking for. Mike found her impossible to resist and before she left to continue her rounds he asked her out to dinner.

68

That moment proved to be the beginning of a love affair that got stronger with each passing month. They began seeing each other regularly, but in different places, each time with Mike coming up with an excuse to be out of town. Mike tried to be as careful as he could. Being a self-made man, he stood to lose everything if he was caught. Murder was never a consideration on his part, given the years and the fact he and Janet had a son.

Actually it was all Jasmine's idea.

She formulated the plan to murder Janet, being quite subtle about it at first, but over time Mike warmed to the idea. He felt trapped, deathly afraid of ruining everything he'd worked so hard for over the years, so he used his knowledge of medicine as well as his meticulous nature to mastermind the crime, and once it had been successfully carried out they began seeing each other more often, but secretly to avoid suspicion.

Jasmine was ruthless. It was she who seduced Charlie while he was in Pittsburgh on business, while Mike took pictures them together at the hotel bar, and after Charlie's death the police found the letters and photographs with the mystery woman in his home exactly as Mike had planned.

Eventually Jasmine had convinced Mike to relocate to the Chicago area. They were married not long thereafter. David, who'd graduated from Northwestern and was now attending the University of California-Berkeley, going after a doctorate in mathematics, wasn't thrilled that his father had moved on with his life. Mike didn't pay it much mind though, for he was fifty-eight years old and feeling better than ever, and to his delight Jasmine expressed interest in having a child together. Things couldn't have been any better; his life had started over.

Everything looked wonderful until the week of Halloween. As the anniversary of his former wife's murder drew close, he became more agitated, anxious. Like Janet at this time three years ago, he also relived her last moments alive over again in his dreams. Quickly these dreams turned to nightmares where he'd search for her in cemeteries, and the old woman in black was always there, menacing him.

Like in the nightmare that he just had.

Chapter Thirteen: To the Morning

October 27, 2001

It was a cold and bitter late October morning in Central Illinois. Driving past Bloomington-Normal proved to be more of a challenge than originally expected for motorists traveling along I-55 north – especially those driving SUVs. One could almost tip over if you weren't careful. The prairies that sprawled across most of this portion of the state couldn't shield one from its high, shrieking winds. In fact, just standing outside for periods of time could cause a person's face to freeze up, making speech very slurred. The kids don't mind that kind of thing. This was the time of the year when playing tackle football in the prairies was best, one of many delights of being raised in the country.

It was too early for kids to throw the pigskin around the fields. It was just after three in the morning, and along the flat four-lane highway a lone motorist from St. Louis was on their way to the western suburbs of Chicago.

The woman had been looking forward to this trip for some time. Her car rolled along on cruise, the stereo played *Believe In Me* by Dan Fogelberg, one of her favorite artists. Rather fitting that she would be listening to his music now, as he was born and raised in nearby Peoria, Illinois. From very simple beginnings his music has long been celebrated by a diverse group of listeners. Songs like *Missing You* and *Run For the Roses* appealed more to a rock audience, while *Longer, Souvenirs* and *Make Love Stay* touched the hearts of country music fans. For years Fogelberg had maintained his popularity because of his versatility. Being an accomplished musician certainly helped – a skill that is all but lost with today's so-called talent.

Another hour and a half before I reach the hotel. Need a break.

She exited I-55 and pulled into a place called Jim's Diner. It wasn't much to look at from the outside, but on the inside it resembled the diner from the old CBS TV show "Alice." She took a quick pit stop, then ordered a cup of black coffee and a cinnamon roll to go. The moment she stepped outside the diner the wind stiffened up her cheeks, so she warmed them up by taking a sip of her coffee while grabbing today's edition of the Chicago Sun-Times from a newspaper stand. She paused, closed her eyes and took a deep breath of the crisp country air. Eventually a thin smile crept across her face.

This will be a good trip.

She climbed back into her car and started the engine, the song *To The Morning* began to play. The soft, gentle piano solo at the beginning made her heart heavy. She reached into her duffel bag in the back seat and took out a photograph, holding it in front of her.

"They're going to pay for what they did to you," she whispered to the woman in the picture. The photo came from the November 7, 1998 edition of the Erie Daily Times.

It was Janet Wilson's obituary.

Chapter Fourteen: Top of the World

Mike drove along the Eisenhower expressway, a ubiquitous melody of the Dave Brubeck Quartet in his ears. The heavy wind and rain made driving very difficult. Not even Mike's $47,000 silver Mercedes Benz E320 sedan could shake off the effects of this weather, and he occasionally found himself holding the steering wheel with both hands – not usually his style. Being from Erie, Mike was used to unpleasant weather. Even at his age he still loved the snow, and Chicago seemed to be a place where there was plenty to go around. My kind of town, indeed.

As 98.7 WFMT Chicago continued to play 'Blue Rondo a la Turk' Mike was lost in thought about a conversation between him and Jasmine regarding the weather. A smile crept across his face as he could picture the scene in his mind. Jas was waiting inside the foyer for him as he pulled into the driveway. He greeted her at the front door with a kiss and was proceeding to take off his coat when she told him to go back outside and park the car in the garage.

"The weatherman is calling for severe weather storms for the next few days, mister!" she said. "You'd better get that car indoors or you'll be soaked tomorrow."

Mike shrugged his shoulders at the thought of going back outside.

"Skip Thompson doesn't have a first clue," he replied.

"Okay, suit yourself," she said, with a look that often meant 'you'll be sorry later, hardhead!'

Mike looked at his trench coat while sitting in the car; it was soaked despite the fact he came outside with an umbrella - now resting on the floor in the backseat with his briefcase. He chuckled to himself at the thought of somewhere a woman named Jas was smirking and saying 'I told you so.'

'You'll be sorry later, hardhead!'

As Mike took the last exit from the Eisenhower he made a quick right onto Ashland Avenue and over to Harrison Street. Rush Hospital began at the corner.

Let the games begin.

Mike loved this part of his trip. He was speeding up to the fourth level of the parking garage, up a circular driveway to his private parking space, making a series of twists and turns. Usually during the last leg of his trip he timed himself, his personal best being twenty-three seconds. It looked clear, so he decided to go for it.

"Today's the day, I can feel it," he thought, as he hit the accelerator.

His tires squealed so loud the casual onlooker would cover their ears, but Mike didn't care. To him, this private race with himself served as a metaphor in his ability to dodge whatever obstacle that lay in his path. U of I basketball, medical school, Janet, it didn't matter – for he'd always found his way despite the odds. He has a new life, a wife whom he loved dearly, and a career that had never been better. Sometimes he thought of himself as Jimmy Cagney in 'White Heat' – one of his favorite movies of all time. Though it seemed like a strange film for one to identify with, he was more focused on Cagney's memorable quote near the end of the film.

Made it, Ma! Top of the world!

Screech! The Mercedes came to a halt square in his parking space. Mike immediately checked his watch – the Rolex;

73

the same one that matched Janet's, which he later turned over to Jasmine. After all, it was originally supposed to be hers anyway.

To J, with love, M.

"DAMN!" Twenty-four seconds; his personal best was still intact. He reached into the back seat and grabbed his briefcase and locked the Mercedes, the 'chirp' sound echoed throughout the garage.

He took a moment to scan the entire area. There were an assortment of sedans, SUV's and small economy cars throughout the floor and past the cars he could see each side of the city off into the distance. The inside of the garage was not insulated from the weather so the wind continued to shriek and drips of rain occasionally hit Mike in the face. Though no one was around Mike still had an eerie feeling, one he couldn't easily shake. He remembered a story Janet told him about Dr. Martin and the nearly damaged cell phone. His lips formed a slight smile.

"You're always there watching me, aren't you?" he whispered to himself.

He made his way toward the elevator and stepped inside once it arrived. Other than the floor, the doors and the instrument panel the inside were clear glass, and despite the rain and the dreary weather outside one could still see the Sears Tower and the John Hancock Center off in the distance.

The wind picked up and caused a whistling sound that deafened the hum of the elevator. Mike realized he'd forgotten his umbrella.

You'll be sorry later, hardhead!

The elevator reached the first level and he immediately pressed 'four' so he could go back for the umbrella. The last thing he needed right now was to walk across the street and come into the office soaking wet. Mike was always early, as he had a ritual where he took ten minutes to review his material, then sit and drink a cup of coffee while listening to music. This was his time to clear his mind and get settled for the upcoming day. Now that was about to be ruined, though one could imagine worse things happening.

Ding. Mike went to his car and reached under the rear seat until he felt his umbrella. As he stood and once again clicked his remote again, he saw a note under his windshield wiper on the driver's side of the car. The hair on his neck stood as they had in his dream the other day. Just then his words from earlier whispered in his ear....

You're always there watching me, aren't you?

As Mike carefully walked around the hood of the Mercedes, a huge knot had formed in his stomach. He suddenly became nauseous though was still relatively steady, his trembling hands reached for the note. What he saw was a sticker of a graveyard scene. In the background were several tombstones, a large moon with silhouettes of bats, a witch on her broomstick, and a tree with no branches with a large gaping hole that looked more like openings for a mouth and eyes. The tree's bare branches had long, sickly looking fingers that could reach out and grab something that came too close.

At the forefront of the scene was a large tombstone with the initials *J.W., R.I.P.* and what appeared to be a ghost rising from a grave. There was also a message: *Boo!* Mike balled up the paper and searched the garage again.

...watching me, aren't you?

Mike heard the elevator doors close and ran to where he could see the ground below.

Someone was in the elevator.

The figure stepped into the pouring rain and made their way toward Harrison Street. They wore a trench coat with black pants underneath and carried a large, light blue umbrella. Halfway down the path, the figure stopped and slowly turned around, They tilted the umbrella down slightly to cover up their face and waved at a surprised Mike, making him feel foolish. It was working.

The figure turned and continued toward Harrison Street, eventually disappearing from sight. All Mike could do was stand there, wondering who that was and why they placed this paper on his windshield.

He looked as if he'd just seen a ghost.

Chapter Fifteen: Oofah!

"Yes sir, that's exactly how it happened, and not too long after I went into the house."

Mike sat back in his brown leather recliner chair, legs propped in the air. He appeared relaxed, a remote in his left hand and a glass of Crown Royal in his right. It was just after six o'clock on October 30th and he was watching the evening news by himself.

Torrential rain had caused severe flooding and power outages in several parts of Cook and DuPage Counties this past week, and this particular segment of CBS news was dedicated to a man who'd recently bought a brand new burgundy Chevrolet Impala SS, only to have it destroyed by a large oak tree in front of his house the following morning. The high wind snapped the tree almost at its base and landed on the man's brand new car parked in the driveway, nearly cutting it in two. The cameraman got a shot of the vehicle from what used to be a hood; it was quite a sight to see. The roof of the Impala was completely bashed in, both the windshield and the rear window were crushed with glass all over the place and the trunk looked as if someone had actually tried to fold it in half; the sides sticking up allowing someone to reach directly into the back without opening the lid. The suspension had collapsed and three of the four tires were blown out. How the front driver side tire was spared, Mike had no idea. Instead he raised his glass as if he were toasting this guy because of some feeling of solidarity he felt. Mike's first car was a Chevy Impala that his father bought for him when he graduated high school in 1961. Mike loved that car and drove it until it was stolen while he was in medical school. He was depressed over that for nearly a month.

"I feel your pain, buddy," Mike said, glass raised in the air as the guy continued on about how he'd only been in the house for a few minutes when the tree fell.

"My wife told me to park it in the garage," the man said. *"I wish I would've listened."*

That caused Mike to smile.

"You'll be sorry later, hardhead!" Mike said, mimicking Jasmine's warning. He chuckled as he watched the screen. "All wives should be weathermen, that's all there is to it."

He took a sip of his drink, hearing the ice *clink* in the glass, which meant it was time for a refill, so he stumbled over to the liquor cabinet and dropped in a few ice cubes.

Mike drank two types of whiskey: Old Overholt and Crown Royal. Overholt was a straight rye whiskey, and since he'd moved to the Midwest he found it hard to locate in Illinois. Crown Royal was more expensive, so he preferred to drink it straight on the rocks. After about two or three glasses he would marvel to Jas about how those *goddamn Canadians make a fine whiskey.* She'd simply giggle at him. To her, Mike was a funny guy...very sexy too. Though he's an older man (Mike was fifty-eight and Jas was thirty-six), he was in top shape. There'd been many a night when he came home and Jas was waiting for him near the door with something seductive on, or sometimes nothing on at all. In many ways she was the perfect temptress; young-looking, beautiful and completely irresistible. It became obvious to many that Mike and Jas were made for each other in more ways than one.

He poured himself another glass. Jas was in Lincoln Park visiting her old sorority sisters Valerie and Dana. The girls got together once or twice a month and either went to dinner or sat

77

at each other's house or apartment and talked about the 'good old days' of being back in school. The three of them pledged Mu Delta Omicron sorority together at the University of Illinois at Chicago and were still active in the city graduate chapter. This was their usual time to reminisce about the days before pledging became illegal or discuss the guys they used to date in other fraternities. Once when Jas was hosting a get together at her house Mike walked in from a long day at work, only to find things becoming very hushed when he came into the room. Their faces all looked as if they were on the verge of laughter, but were desperately trying to hold it in, looking like teenagers trying to cover up something when the parents unexpectedly walked into the room. Several empty bottles of Chardonnay and containers of Chinese food could usually be found scattered around on the living room floor. General Tso's chicken, shrimp fried rice and dumplings were the usual staple of gossipers up to no good.

"Hello Mike," they'd say in unison. And as soon as Mike left the room they'd burst out in laughter, which indeed they did. Mike smiled as he walked upstairs. He'd be lying if he said that didn't make him feel good.

In fact, he loved all the attention he could get.

Mike took a sip of his drink, remembering that Jas had asked him to go up to the attic and get his costume ready for Valerie's annual Halloween costume party tomorrow night. Though Mike loved parties he wasn't much for changing costumes. He was a horror movie fanatic, and since Bela Lugosi and Christopher Lee were his two favorite horror film actors, he always dressed as Dracula.

"Why change what works?" he would always say, much to Jasmine's chagrin. Eventually she gave up trying to change his mind.

***

Mike grabbed his drink and made his way to the attic. Their town home was four levels high if you included the loft that overlooked the master bedroom. When you walked into their room to the right was the staircase, and upstairs they had the loft as a makeshift attic, filled with boxes and papers stacked

78

neatly in a storage room separate from the rest of the floor. Also in the storage room Mike built a two-person sauna, which he used after working out on his bow-flex machine. The open space had been turned into a home office that only Mike used. Jas had an office of her own, located down on the ground floor next to the den.

Behind a large mahogany desk against the wall stood two matching bookshelves with books and articles ranging from the *Psychiatric News* to *Beyond Good and Evil* by Friedrich Nietzsche. Very recently Mike published a series of articles in the International College of Psychiatrists and was working on his second book, *Psychiatry of the Twenty-First Century*, a book focused on the history and evolution of psychiatric care to the present day, along with a culmination of case studies that he'd performed over the years as well as an in-depth discussion of the direction of psychiatry in the new millennium. Mike submitted a treatment for his book to a few publishing companies almost a year ago and received a stipend of $10,000 from DTB Medical Publishers, who eagerly awaited the finished product. Mike anticipated he'd have the book finished in six months.

Mike placed his drink by his new laptop and searched through stacked boxes in the storage area. Each box was marked on the side, so he knew he wouldn't have much trouble finding what he was looking for. While he continued his search he came to a box marked *photos and documents* and decided to take a look. It was stuffed with scrap albums, old final exams for his students at Loyola, and David's high school and college diplomas. David chose to give them to his father since his dad helped him get through school. Little did David know Mike was about to mail them to Berkeley as part of his Christmas gift.

Their relationship had initially taken a beating with Mike getting remarried so soon, but as he opened one of the scrapbooks Mike remembered how things had recently come together between them in a very inspirational way.

***

One day while Mike was driving home to Wheaton he got a call from Jas, who remarked that she needed to speak with him about something important. He asked her what was wrong, but she mentioned this needed to be done in person.

Mike pulled into the driveway and found Jas waiting for him in the living room. Except for a candle lit on the coffee table it was dark inside the house. Mike was a little puzzled why she was sitting in darkness, but it was obvious whatever she had to say was important. He sat down on the couch next to her very quietly just as she explained to him the reason she wanted to talk to him face to face. It was regarding David. She mentioned she had received a phone call from him while at work stating he had something to share with his father that he was very afraid to. Jas went on to explain that David was gay and recently came out of the closet while living in California. She also mentioned that David was happily living with his life partner, Adam Carlson, who was an associate professor of economics at the university. They met through the Lesbian, Gay, Bisexual and Transgender Services Office on campus, where Adam served as the faculty advisor for the organization. Normally it was not Adam's style to ask out a student, but with David being older than the average student he took a chance, to which David said yes. Though ten years apart in age (David was thirty-one, Adam was forty-one), they had so much in common and loved each other dearly. The couple had recently celebrated their first year together and decided it was time to make their love official. They were planning a small commitment ceremony in San Francisco, and both men wanted their families to attend. In David's case, if he truly wanted his father to attend and be involved in his life, they needed to resolve their individual issues.

Mike openly wept, not from disappointment, but from the fact that his son was happy and thought enough of him to want to be honest about his sexuality.

"There's something else you need to know," Jas said, gesturing towards the front of the house. "David is outside and won't come in unless the lights come on. If it stays out that means our discussion didn't go well."

Barely waiting for her to say anything else, Mike turned on every light on the first level and raced to the front door, his son standing in the driveway. Mike ran and hugged him, tears streaming down his face. He released his grip and placed his hands behind David's neck.

"Davey, you're my son and I love you!" Mike said.

"I love you too dad," replied David, now crying as well, relieved that his dad hadn't shunned him. "By the way, I have someone I want you to meet."

Adam, David's partner, approached them. He was a tall man, about six foot four, well groomed and wearing a white button down long sleeve shirt, navy blue jeans and Rockport shoes. Mike extended his right hand gesturing for Adam to join them. Both men shook hands.

"Welcome to the family," Mike said.

"May I call you dad?" Adam quipped. Both men laughed.

"Hey guys, how about a picture?" Jas asked, standing in the driveway with her camera. Father, son and son-in-law turned and posed for the camera.

Flash!

***

Mike sniffled as the wonderful memories came back to him. He and Jas went to visit them in August and had a wonderful time. There were several photos of them together touring San Francisco, visiting The Presidio, Golden Gate Park, Castro Street and Alcatraz Island. Everyone had a lovely time, and Mike couldn't wait to make another trip out there again after the holidays. Plane tickets had already been reserved.

It was times like these that caused Mike to ever so slightly regret murdering his wife.

Mike continued looking through photographs when he heard *Oofah!* come from his computer. Mike was a big Sopranos fan, and his favorite character on the show was Paulie Walnuts, so he downloaded sound bytes from the Sopranos home page and substituted them for the regular AOL jingles. Mike often left his instant messenger running in case it was a colleague or a student that needed to get in touch with him.

He walked over to the computer and sat at the desk, grabbed his whiskey. The person who IM'd him was Jas - her screen name was *MsMystery*. Mike grinned as he took a sip.

MsMystery: Hey sexy, are you there?

Psychedoc: Yep, I'm right here — looking for my costume in the attic.
MsMystery: Cool — I'm sitting here thinking about what we can do when I come home!
Psychedoc: I know what we can do — we can play 'musical beds' when you get back!
MsMystery: Musical Beds?
Psychedoc: Yeah, you know, games like 'pin the cock in the beauty'? LOL

Mike picked up his glass and took another sip waiting for Jas' response.

MsMystery: Now that sounds like an idea! I'll be the beauty!

Mike accidentally dropped his drink onto the hardwood floor. Crown Royal and ice splattered everywhere.

"Shit!" Mike shouted, looking at what he'd just done. He searched the area for something to clean the mess he made.

"Oofah!" Mike looked at the screen.

MsMystery: What happened?   Are you alright?

Mike wiped his hands on his shorts and was about to type when he realized he was *typing*, not talking. His hands shook. The hairs on the back of his neck stood up.

Psychedoc: Jas, are you in the house???
MsMystery: Yes, but I have a confession to make!
Psychedoc: What's that?

Mike sat perfectly still, enough to hear his heart beating as he looked to his right in the direction of the storage room. He heard a flutter in his breathing.

Thump, thump! Thump, thump!

MsMystery: I confess that I'm not Jasmine."

Mike felt a cold shiver go down his back. He pushed away from his desk, hands gripping the leather arms of his chair. His stomach felt queasy.

"Oofah!" Mike got closer to the screen so he could see.

MsMystery: I'm baaaaaaaaaaack!

Mike heard a crash from the ground floor and ran so fast he nearly tripped down the stairs. Past the kitchen. Down the steps. Through the foyer. Down the hall. The wind from the outside storm picked up as he carefully searched for the wall light switch, flicking it on. Jasmine's office been trashed; papers and books from the bookshelves were all over the floor, a garbage can was overturned, Jasmine's desk was disheveled.

82

The only thing that was undisturbed was a picture frame containing a photograph of Mike and Jasmine on their wedding day.

Mike began to fear the worst, and given what he'd done to Janet and Charlie, he decided to not discuss this with anyone. The only thing he did know for certain was someone was coming for him. But whom?

"...watching me, aren't you?"

Chapter Sixteen: Gift Ideas

The storm raged on through most of the next day. Jas spent some of her afternoon out shopping, trying to help Valerie get a few last minute details together for her costume party. Trudging through the inclement weather was no big deal for a sorority sister. As one could see with Mike, Jas was fiercely loyal to people she cared for, and especially to Dana and Valerie with whom she pledged way back when.

"A sorors' work is never done!" she often said, and to her there were no two ways about it.

Mike went with Jas to Costco and stood by as she filled a rather large shopping card with items for the party. His approach to shopping was much simpler. Though he had great taste for most other things he tended to stick more to Triscuit Crackers and block cheddar cheese as serving items for hors d'eouvres. Being with Jas was indeed a welcomed learning experience for him. Though Mike spent a portion of his childhood years in Cleveland and his early adulthood in Philadelphia, he was used to the creature comforts of Erie, Pennsylvania. Jas was breaking him out of his shell in ways that Janet never had. Sometimes he wondered what life would've been like had he met Jasmine first. Would he have brought forth a child like David, whom he was so proud of? Would he have attained a level of success earlier in his life that he has now?

Would he ultimately have killed Jasmine for someone else? Perhaps not, but then again – one never knows.

Having grown rather bored of looking at party favors Mike decided to take off on his own for a while with Jas's blessing. Across the street from Costco was River Forest Mall, so he decided to walk around there for a while. He was looking for a new jogging suit and a pair of sneakers, so he thought he'd try MC Mages Sporting Goods and Foot Locker, both of which had their outlet stores in the mall.

As expected, Mike found the mall filled to the gills with kids dressed in costumes. It almost seemed that if the kids weren't wearing a costume they were on their way to a toy store to buy one. One boy seemed to literally drag his mother into nearby K-Bee Toys, which was right next to Foot Locker.

"Mommy, c'mon Mommy," the child exclaimed, pulling his mother's right arm. Kids can be awfully strong when they want to be.

Mike smiled as he stood in front of Foot Locker, looking at a flustered parent forced against her will going into the store. It reminded him of times when he and Janet took David shopping for Halloween. Those were fun days indeed. David loved Halloween, and he was rather creative with his costumes and would sometimes make his own. In high school he put together a presentation for his English teacher where he discussed the origin of Halloween. Dressed as a druid priest, he explained to the class that Halloween comes from the Celtic name *Samhain*, pronounced *Sow-in* in Ireland, which stood for "summer's end." Beginning at sundown on October 31st it was believed that the spirit world and the living were closest during this time and the dead would visit their living kinfolk. Many would leave milk and cakes outside their doors or set an extra space at the table for any relatives that passed in case they wanted to join the living for dinner.

Druid priests celebrated the Festival of Samhain as a special holiday. Needless to say, David dressing up in a costume while making his presentation added to the effect. He got an A for his hard work, along with many accolades from his teacher and fellow classmates. He and Janet spent many long hours working on this project.

Mike passed by Foot Locker for the moment and went next door into Kay-Bee Toys. Eventually he ran into the boy and the mother, who were standing in front of the mirror profiling some costumes. They seemed to settle on a red, white and blue clown outfit, which came with a matching mask that had a big red nose. The boy seemed happy with his choice.

Mike continued down the second aisle and came to a selection of Jack-in-the-Boxes that were eye level across the shelves. There were ten different types, including the classic 'Bozo the Clown' version from 1971, similar to the ones he purchased for David as a young toddler. He picked one up and sang the tune to Pop Goes the Weasel until Bozo popped out of the hatch, his plastic, gangly arms extended.

Just like the ones sold when David was a child, this clown wore a blue outfit with white polka dots and had red hair, a pink nose and lips and streaks of blue around the eyes. Bozo's box still resembled the original one; however the box itself was not the original tin like in its earlier years. Now it was packaged in plastic – more than likely as a safety measure for kids. Mike found it interesting in this day and age that they would still manufacture one that closely resembled the original. Jas actually liked to collect old toys and had a bookshelf in her office dedicated to ones she had as a child. She had almost four-dozen toys in her collection, including a tin kaleidoscope, an old McDonald music radio, an etch-a-sketch and the original Mr. Potato Head. She did mention that she wanted a Jack-in-the-Box, so Mike decided to buy it for her as a Christmas gift.

"She'll love this," he thought as he walked to the checkout aisle near the front of the store.

Mike stood waiting as the young boy tried to drag away his mother once again. She'd just given her credit card to the cashier and was signing the receipt. The boy jumped up and down, excited that he had the costume he wanted. Mike smiled at them once again, watching them turn a corner around the store's entrance, eventually disappearing from view.

He checked his watch. One-thirty in the afternoon.

"I'll have to hurry," he thought.

A woman stood in the busy corridor outside the store looking at him. She'd been following him since he entered the mall, observing him as he looked around the toy store. Seeing all that she wanted, she walked quickly towards the security office at the end of the mall corridor. Mike was nearing the front of the line when he heard something come over the PA system outside: *"Paging Dr. Mike Wilson, Paging Dr. Mike Wilson.....your wife is waiting for you at the security office on the first level. Dr. Wilson, your wife is waiting for you at the security office. Thank you."*

"I've gotta go," he explained to the cashier. Figuring it was Jas Mike knew he couldn't take her gift with him, so he handed it to the cashier and left the store.   At the security office he found a man sitting behind a desk filling out paperwork. He was wearing a navy blue sport coat, white shirt and black tie with gray slacks. On his coat was a security badge and on the right sleeve of his coat was an oval-shaped embroidered patch that said "River Forest Mall" written in cursive print below what appeared to be an evergreen tree. Mike could see the security guard's badge – *J.Wall.*

"Hi, can I help you?"

"Yes, I'm Dr. Wilson. I believe you paged me over your PA system."

"Oh yes, lost were you?" the guard quipped, his mouth forming a smile.

"Hardly," Mike chuckled. "I'm looking for my wife. Where is she?"

The guard looked around. He frowned as he looked towards the empty chairs in the waiting area.

"That's funny, she was just here a second ago," he said. "She was sitting right by the doors."

He was pointing towards a chair that had a 'People' magazine sitting on it. Mike joined the security guard with a frowned look on his face. He reached in his pocket for his cell phone, dialing Jas' number.

"Hello?"

"Hey babe, where are you?" Mike asked anxiously.

"Where else? Stuck in line here at K-Mart. Of all the lines I have to be in, it has to be one with a new cashier. Did you get your jogging suit?"

"Oh...uh, not yet. Sorry, I thought I saw you here a second ago," Mike replied. "I'll see you shortly." He hung up without waiting for a response.

"What did this woman look like?" he asked.

The guard went on to describe someone who looked like the woman he saw at the parking lot a few days ago. Mike thanked the guard, then headed back into the main corridor, hurriedly walking towards the parking lot. The guard chuckled as he watched Mike walk away, looking around as if he were trying to keep from being seen. To the onlooker he appeared paranoid that someone was following him.

Chapter Seventeen: Party Time

Halloween

The following morning Mike and Jasmine had started their day at roughly nine that morning and had finished by mid-afternoon, both wet from the storm and exhausted from the constant walking, fighting crowds and standing in lines. Valerie's parties always began late, so there was enough time to take a short nap, get into costume and head to the north side of the city. She lived on Fullerton Avenue, nearby DePaul University where she's taught English Literature for the past eight years. Recently divorced and no children, she was intent on publishing a non-fiction book regarding the life and death of Emmett Till.

Valerie had been fascinated with this tragedy since college and five years ago she began researching the subject in detail, interviewing family members and reading transcripts of the trial. Very recently she'd completed her book, totaling nearly four hundred pages and after obtaining an agent she had been playing the waiting game with several publishers. To date there have been no responses.

After napping until six that evening, Mike and Jasmine rose and began dressing in their costumes. Since Mike has worn his costume many times before, Jas tried to change her look with each year. The last two years she's gone as both Cinderella and Tinker Bell from Peter Pan, but this year she chose something a little more provocative: *Elvira, Mistress of the Dark.* She figured since Mike refused to go as anything but Dracula, she may as well match her costume to his this year. And since Jas fit Elvira's tight black dress quite well, it seemed like a perfect match. Of course Mike enjoyed looking at his wife privately wearing such an outfit, but since she was going to be in public he kept walking after Jas with a black shawl insisting she wear it when in the company of men at the party. All this did was cause Jasmine to shake her head and laugh.

"Men are such fragile creatures, aren't they?" she would often say. At times Mike was living proof.

They made their way to the garage and hopped in the Mercedes in full costume. This would surely cause people to stop and stare while standing at a red light in traffic. In many ways Mike transformed into Count Dracula once the costume was on and a few times bared his fangs at nosey people pointing at them until the light turned green. Once he even acted as if he was biting Elvira's neck to the astonishment of an elderly couple that gawked at them. As they screeched their 1965 Chrysler Newport through the intersection all Jas could do was giggle. Mike could be such a child at times, which was one of his most endearing qualities as far as she was concerned.

The storm had lightened up a bit as they arrived near Valerie's condo. Mike found a parking spot for the Mercedes on Belden Avenue and grabbed the bags with the food and plates, making their way toward Fullerton.

The sidewalks were matted with leaves and broken tree branches. Mike noticed several parents steering their trick-or-treating kids around huge puddles of water. Puddles and kids are like metal and magnets – they just seem to attract one another, and despite the valiant efforts of the parents, the kids still managed to splash water everywhere. Memories of taking David out trick or treating brought a smile to Mike's face. He and Janet would help him dress up in his favorite costume of the year, whichever one it was, for it changed with each passing Halloween. The only costume David wore more than once was

Casper the Friendly Ghost. He and Janet would sit together on Saturday mornings and watch the cartoon, and when the show began Janet and David would sing the show's opening jingle. Janet was such a good mother to David, who still misses her to this day. Mike could never tell him what he had done. This was the only guilt Mike had for orchestrating Janet's murder – he would lose his only son whom he loved.

The wind picked up as they rounded onto Fullerton Avenue, and headed into Valerie's building. They waited patiently by the elevator for the doors to open, and from the lobby Mike could see the car begin its descent from the eleventh floor, which was where they were headed.

The doors opened. Mike and Jasmine, bags in hand, stepped inside when suddenly a figure stormed out of the elevator, knocking packages out of Mike's hand.

"Hey – watch where you're going!" Mike snapped, picking up his bags. Jas had a disgusted look on her face.

The figure, wearing a tan trench coat over what resembled the hood of a light blue sweat suit, passed both of them and kept walking through the lobby, unconcerned about the packages they had knocked over and continued walking through the double glass doors onto Fullerton. Mike shook his head and shuffled the bags into the elevator while Jas pressed the button for the eleventh floor.

***

They entered the crowded living room, 'A Night in Tunisia' by Charlie "Bird" Parker played softly in the background. Valerie was a huge fan of Jazz, as were most people from the Chicago area. Blues and Jazz dominated the music scene of the City, especially the area in which she lived. Within walking distance of her apartment were several clubs with live entertainment available for anyone that was interested. Whenever they came over for a visit Mike took time to marvel at her CD collection, and this time was no exception. After hauling the bags into the kitchen he walked to the entertainment center to do an inventory of her newest discs. Jas came and tapped him on the shoulder.

91

"Sweetie, I'm going into the bedroom to help Valerie get her outfit on. I'll be right back", she said. Mike nodded, redirecting his gaze back at her collection.

"Hello there stranger," a voice called from behind him.

Mike looked into the smiling face of Dana Evers, one of the Mu Delta 'Three Amigos.' She was a lovely woman: five-foot six inches tall, long black hair and sparkling brown eyes. Like Jas and Valerie, she had a very fine figure. Her face and bubbly personality reminded him of Janet Jackson, and she was every bit as attractive. She worked as an investment banker for Bank of America in downtown Chicago and was quite successful at her job. Oddly enough though, Mike noticed she wasn't dressed in costume at all, for she was wearing jeans and a DePaul University sweatshirt. Though she was definitely "all-woman," she also was fierce martial arts student and taught classes in jiujutsu at the Lincoln Park YWCA. Mike often thought God help the man that cheated on this woman, for there would be hell to pay.

"Hey sweetheart, great to see you!" Mike replied. "How long have you been here?" Mike gave her a hug and kiss.

"Been here all afternoon getting things ready, so now it's time for me to get into my costume, which seems to have disappeared," she replied, looking around the crowded room. "Strange, but I thought I brought it here with me earlier."

"Don't worry, you'll find it! What kind of costume is it?"

"Ah ah, Mike!" she returned sharply, holding up her index finger. "That's for me to know and you to find out!"

"I can't wait," Mike replied, smiling, hands raised in the air.

Dana laughed.

"Be back in a few, dear – and love the costume."

She gently stroked Mike's arm, then made her way toward the front closet. Mike watched as she put on her coat, and then went through the front door towards the elevator. He felt in his heart there was some chemistry between them. Dana clearly was his type, but Mike thought it best to leave it where it stood. Besides, Jas would kill him if he ever looked at another woman, let alone her best friend. She'd already helped him kill

Janet, so he was smart enough to know it gets easier the second time around.

Chapter Eighteen: Mystery Woman

Nearly an hour had passed and Mike continued to wander around the room, talking to a few of Valerie's guests. Many of the people were professional – some doctors and lawyers, educators and city officials. There were a few city workers there as well, in addition to some graduate students from DePaul. Valerie was a well-rounded young woman who knew a lot of people, and though there was a wide range of folks in attendance they all seemed to be down to earth and very friendly, just like she was. Mike liked that about Jasmine. She had great friends who really welcomed him in as one of their own.

Mike checked his watch; it was nearly ten o'clock. He hadn't seen Jas since they arrived, and Dana had returned from her car with the missing costume and went to Valerie's bedroom to get dressed. He shook the glass in his hand, usually a sign that it was time for a refill, so he approached the bar for more Crown Royal. Valerie had hired a bartender and had a wide assortment of drinks available. Mike stuck with what he knew best. Why change what works?

"Crown Royal on the rocks, please," he said to the bartender. He stuffed a five dollar bill in the tip jar.

He took a sip of CR and took in the sounds of Miles Davis' *A Kind of Blue* when a costumed person wearing a strange looking Chinese mask approached the bar. This person wore a beautiful light blue silk robe with a matching sash around the waist. Embroidered on the sleeve of the robe were several inscriptions that appeared to be written in Chinese, and on the back was a beautifully stitched design of a dragon with a bright red sun in the background. The person wore thin white socks and very eloquent looking sandals that matched the color of the robe. The mask, however, looked gnarled and ugly, appearing to represent an evil spirit. In a weird kind of way, the outfit seemed to denote a figure of royalty that was to be feared and yet oddly admired. This immediately caught Mike's attention and he wondered whether this was someone from the Ming Dynasty.

"Seven and seven, please" the muffled voice said from behind the mask. The voice sounded that of a woman, but Mike couldn't tell for sure.

The figure looked at Mike then back to the bartender, who handed over the glass. They placed a ten dollar bill in the tip jar, then inserted a straw into the glass and took a sip through the slit where the mouth was on the mask. Mike continued to be very intrigued by the horribly disfigured mask and turned to face the costumed figure.

"That's a fantastic outfit you have on," he said. "What is it supposed to mean?"

"Why thank you," the figure replied, whom Mike clearly identified as a woman.

"I'm wearing what's known as a Chinese totem mask," she continued. "This particular one is called 'Shi-tien yen-wang.' Have you ever heard of that?"

Mike shook his head. The woman continued.

"The Shi-tien Yen-Wang were known in Mythology as the Lords of Death, the nine rulers of the underworld. They dress alike in royal robes and only the wisest can tell them apart. Each ruler presides over one court of law."

Mike appeared totally fascinated.

"Are you following me so far?" She paused, waiting for a response.

"Please continue."

"In the first court a soul is judged according to his sins in life and sentenced to one of the eight courts of punishment. Punishment is fitted to the offense. Misers are made to drink molten gold; liars' tongues are cut out. In the second court are incompetent doctors and dishonest agents; in the third, forgers, liars, gossips, and corrupt government officials; in the fourth, murderers, in the fifth are sex offenders and atheists; in the sixth, the sacrilegious and blasphemers; in the seventh, those guilty of filial disrespect; in the eighth, arsonists and accident victims. In the ninth is the Wheel of Transmigration where souls are released, then reincarnated after their punishment is completed. Before souls are released, they are given a brew of oblivion, which makes them forget their former lives."

"Wow, so are you a student of Chinese history?"

"Uh huh. In fact I teach it at Washington University in Saint Louis. I just happen to be here for the weekend and am visiting a friend at DePaul who knows Valerie. Lovely party, isn't it?"

"Yes indeed, my wife is somewhere helping Val into her costume. She's been gone for a while though. I wonder what in the hell she's up to."

"I'm sure whatever Val is wearing, it's going to be extravagant," the woman said.

Mike took another sip of Crown Royal. His focus went back to this woman's costume.

"So let me ask you a question, if there are nine rulers of the underworld and you can only tell each other apart, then which court do you preside over?"

The woman turned and looked at him. She placed her drink on the bar counter.

"I preside over the first court, where I astutely judge the sins of men, and alone have the power to sentence you to one of the remaining eight courts of punishment. Though I consider myself to be a fair judge I also show no mercy for the wicked. The punishment will undoubtedly fit the crime."

The hairs on Mike's neck stood again. The woman's voice deepened as she spoke, and suddenly all he heard were the words that came from her mouth. She came closer to him, her brown eyes looking through the mask directly into his.

"What about you? Have you done something that you should be judged for in my courtroom?"

Her eyes never blinked as she spoke. Mike looked directly at her, then down at the floor as he carefully prepared his response. Her sternness only caused him to feel shame for the grave sin he had committed a few years earlier.

"Nothing that my wife wouldn't kill me for," he said, chuckling at the irony of his response.

The woman stepped back, eyes still not blinking. Suddenly a rather wicked laugh came from behind the mask. Mike smiled, and though the sound was muffled, he could almost swear he'd heard this woman's voice before. He wanted to say something else to her, and it was then he realized he didn't know her name. He felt funny because he also realized he hadn't properly introduced himself either, not like his normally polite demeanor. Up to now she still hadn't removed her mask.

"I'm sorry, I should've introduced myself to you. My name is Mike Wilson," he said, extending his hand.

The woman's handshake was firm. And after her release, she made a crisp turn and walked away, leaving Mike completely bewildered. She headed towards the bathroom and closed the door.

Mike looked at the bartender. "Was it something I said?"

He shrugged. "With women, one never knows."

***

Mike was about to order another drink when he saw Jasmine standing over by the entertainment center in the living room trying to get everyone's attention. His watch read 10:13 pm.

"Excuse me everyone, but I'd like to introduce to you your host for this evening, Miss Satin Doll!"

The music to Duke Ellington's "Satin Doll" played and out walked Valerie dressed in gold from head to toe, resembling an African queen. Her outfit and makeup were impeccably done, and as she headed towards the living room she danced very seductively. She was greeted with a hearty round of applause

97

from her guests. Dana stood next to her dressed as a playboy bunny. She certainly had the body of one.

"Everyone, I'm glad to see you're having a good time. And as we get closer to the witching hour I hope you'll have an even greater time," Val said, as the music continued. "Please, please, my house is your house!"

Mike took his fresh drink and searched for the woman in the mask. He pushed his way through the crowd and came to the bathroom by the front door. It was opened, but the light was off. He turned on the light and saw the light blue robe and mask sitting on the toilet seat.

There was no sign of the woman anywhere.

***

The mystery woman, now wearing the trench coat and light blue sweatshirt she wore earlier when she bumped into Mike and Jasmine, stood look on Fullerton Avenue, surveying the block. She checked her watch. Ten-thirty.

"Plenty of time."

She looked up into the night sky toward Valerie's apartment, thinking how fun it was to get so close to Mike without giving herself away.

"Soon it will all be over," she thought as she drove along Lake Shore Drive, heading casually towards her destination.

Wheaton, Illinois.

Chapter Nineteen: Stormy Night

Not long after eleven it began raining heavily, and after midnight the news announced there was a tornado watch in effect for several nearby counties. Most people had wisely decided to remain indoors, but there were a few, like Mike and Jasmine, who stayed out longer than they should have. A major power outage hit the City of Wheaton. Whole neighborhoods had been shrouded in complete darkness, the only interruption being a lone car driving cautiously along the roads until it found its way into a driveway.

Mike put on the brakes, realizing that the garage door wouldn't open because the power was down. He looked at Jasmine with a slight expression of disgust.

"Shit Jas, we're gonna have to make a run for it!" he said. "Power's out here too."

"Alrightie. Let's go for it!" she said, equally not happy about stepping out into the rain with her Elvira costume.

He parked as close to the house as possible, then nodded. They both rushed out the car and were completely soaked by the time they made it to the front door. Mike rushed through his ring of keys and finally unlocked the door, stepping inside. The both of them were so wet they could peel off their costumes like one would peel a banana. They stood close to one another, shivering.

"My, my Count, but you're awfully wet behind the ears," Jasmine said, looking as bad as he was.

Getting back into character, Mike reached into his pocket and put his fangs in his mouth, then said: "Yes, and I want to bite your neck and give you a hickey. Blah, Blah!"

Mike covered her in his long, soaked cape. Jas shrieked. Water flew everywhere. They both almost slipped standing on the ceramic tile in the foyer.

"Since we don't have power, what'd say we end this night with a nice fire and some champagne?" Mike asked.

"Sounds like a great idea," Jasmine replied. "You get the fire going, and I'll get the champagne."

He kissed her, then opened the closet by the front door and reached for a flashlight.

***

Mike had changed into dry clothing and was heading downstairs to start the fire. Jasmine hadn't finished changing her clothes, so he handed her his flashlight and got another one from the upstairs hall closet. Fortunately he'd taken the precaution of making sure each floor in their four-floor town home had working flashlights in case of a power outage.

He made it down to the living room, grabbed a few logs from the basket and twisted up a few pieces of paper. Within minutes there was a nice fire and the sweet redolence of birch wood filled the room.

"Jas, if you want I'll grab the champagne!" he shouted, hoping she was able to hear him.

"Go ahead, I'll be right down!" Jasmine answered.

Mike went to the kitchen and grabbed a bottle of Dom Perignon from the refrigerator. He grabbed two champagne glasses from the cabinet, filled his wine bucket with ice and brought everything back to the living room.

Everything was ready. He called again for Jasmine.

"Jas, I'm all set up! Come on down, and you'd better be naked!" he said smiling.

A series of bumping noises came from upstairs. He figured it was Jasmine running into furniture on her way down.

"Boy, we're graceful this evening," he chuckled.

Mike continued to stroke the fire, the embers sputtered and popped with each poke. He looked out the living room window. The storm was still pretty nasty outside. He leaned against the fireplace mantle and felt something touch his shoulder. He picked up the object and held it in front of the fire so he could see.

It was a Jack-in-the-Box, and on it was a note that said *turn*.

"What in the world?" he thought.

Mike scanned the toy, took a deep breath and started to turn the crank very slowly. He could hear the flutter in his breathing as he began.

"All along the winding road...

Mike paused. The hairs on his neck stood up again. A cold chill rushed through his body. Feeling as if he were close to fainting, he turned the crank again.

"...in and out the steeple...that's how the story goes ..."

He paused again. It was clear he didn't want to do this, but somehow he felt compelled to continue.

"...pop goes the weasel."

Out came a headless Bozo. Someone had cut the head of the clown off the rest of the body, leaving his polka-dot blue suit ripped and small metal springs sticking through the opening. On the suit someone taped a folded piece of paper.

It read: *She's next!*

Mike dropped the box and called Jasmine again:

"Jas!" he said. "Babe, are you alright?"

No answer.

Mike grabbed his flashlight and ran to the staircase, tension rising in his chest with each step. At the top of the stairs he played his flashlight across the floor. The hall wasn't as long as the house in Erie, but there was nearly as many rooms. Like the downstairs, the entire second level had hardwood floors. Mike could see the door to the guestroom, usually closed, was now wide-open and wet footprints came out making a trail down the hallway and into the master bedroom.

"Jas, are you alright?" No response.

He followed the trail into the bedroom. Using his flashlight he searched the room for Jas, when he noticed something else. The bed was still made, though there were signs of struggle and blood appeared to be smeared across the quilt, the headboard and the floor. Most of the blood had pooled up near the nightstand, then made a trail into the bathroom, as if someone had been dragging a body. He walked into the bathroom, still following the blood. There was a *drip, drip* sound coming from the sink. The bloody trail continued along the tiled floor until it reached the cabinet. Mike could see a foot, and the dripping sound was not the faucet, but blood that was dripping onto the floor. It was Jasmine. She had been carefully placed onto the bathroom sink with her back against the mirror, and her head was leaning off to the side.

"Jesus!" Mike screamed.

He took a step back and slipped on Jasmine's blood, landing on his back. Dazed, he dropped the flashlight and it rolled from left to right, revealing a pair of feet standing in the darkness in front of him. Lightning revealed the figure of a woman standing in front of him in a white, tattered, mud-ridden dress. She had a knife in her right hand.

"Janet!" Mike gasped.

The shape reached toward him, but he managed to crawl by her and get out of the bathroom. Mike struggled to his feet and went for the stairs.

Thump, thump! Thump, thump!

The corpse following close behind. The storm was at its peak.

Thump, thump! Thump, thump!

Mike collapsed against the banister as the shape rushed after him, knife held above her head. He fell down the staircase and he struck his head against the hardwood floor.

He was convinced that Janet had returned from the grave to make him pay for what he did to her. Gibberish came out of his mouth. His entire body began to flail about, as the shape

102

came down the stairs. He vomited all over himself as he crawled into a corner, shaking his head in disbelief and curling into a fetal position.

Mike had gone completely mad. A rush of disjointed memories from the previous thirty years came at him so fast that he was unable to stop them, all flashing like an intermittent beam of light in the face of this woman he once loved. In what little remained of his mind, he begged this ghost to leave him, but only a stream of gibberish and spittle came from his lips.

The figure came closer and knelt down next to him, removing her wig. The woman in the tattered dress was not Janet at all. Instead it was *Regina*, the little girl from Janet's mirror, only Regina was now grown up. Mike was as correct as he could have been for thinking it was Janet, for Regina was Janet's twin sister - the sister she never knew existed!

Chapter Twenty: Angelina Channing

Margaret Hampton invited a young woman by the name of Ariel into her home for a cup of tea. She was pleasant, but odd as she was dressed entirely in black, from the color of her hair to her shoes. The two of them sat alone and talked for hours, and after seeing pictures and hearing stories about the little girl she gave away, Ariel handed Margaret a special gift for her daughter – the handheld mirror. As luck would have it, just an hour later Ariel would see her daughter for the first and only time on the school bus later that day.

In the fall of 1996 Regina found Ariel shortly before she died. For many years prior she desired to know more about her blood-related family, so she attempted in earnest to locate them. After requesting her adoption papers from the State of Pennsylvania she discovered she was born at Saint Vincent's Hospital for Unwed Mothers in Philadelphia, not Saint Eligius Hospital as originally told to her by her adoptive parents. Though Regina knew there was no malicious intent on their part to mislead her, she still was quite upset to find out she'd been wrong about where she was born after all this time.

Since a new birth certificate was issued when Regina was adopted, she demanded to see the original and found her mother's true name was Angelina Channing. Regina hired an investigator to locate Angelina, and eventually they found her in Lancaster, Pennsylvania where she was a member of the Shining Moon Society of Witches, where for a long time she lived as Ariel, the high priestess in a group of thirteen members, a traditional number in a coven.

After finally having the chance to meet her mother she learned that Angelina gave birth to twins and that Janet was not just an imaginary person, but she was indeed real. Ashamed that she had given her children away, Angelina managed to find both adoptive parents years later and gave each one a hand held mirror. Each mirror had a magic spell placed upon it by Angelina so that the girls would be able to communicate with one another, hoping that one day Janet and Regina would someday find each other. Angelina's wish was beginning to come true.

Two years later Regina found that Janet lived in Erie and came to the house where her sister lived on October 31st, only to arrive too late. Mike had already covered up his crime.

A murder committed by a wolf in sheep's clothing.

***

Regina decided to rehire the investigator who found Angelina to look into the circumstances of Janet's death. What he found was that Charlie, her sister's next door neighbor, was suspected of having an a brief affair with a younger woman, and from the police report he obtained there was evidence that her sister allegedly knew about it, as there were photos taken of Charlie and the unknown woman at a hotel restaurant in Pittsburgh. The investigator managed to obtain copies of the photographs, which clearly showed their faces, and gave them to her, along with a copy of the report. It appeared to her that Janet was blackmailing Charlie, but something didn't seem right to her about this. Why would Janet do it when she clearly didn't need the money? Was Mike somehow involved? Were they both in on it together and somehow Charlie found out? There were a lot of questions going through Regina's mind, for this entire thing didn't make sense, but with no other leads she decided to put it out of her mind for now.

A little over a year ago Regina was on vacation in Chicago visiting her old college roommates from UIC. One morning they all decided to go to breakfast at Lou Mitchell's restaurant on Jackson Boulevard, near the historic Union Station. Regina was reading the Sunday Edition of the Chicago Tribune and skimmed through Weddings and Engagements when she saw the announcement of an engagement between Dr. Michael Wilson and Ms. Jasmine Kaye. She stared at the photograph of the two of them together; Mike beamed proudly in his tuxedo, and Jasmine wore a beautiful white silk blouse and a gold necklace with a heart shaped locket around her neck. Mike was holding her left hand, which revealed a beautiful diamond ring, very similar to the one he gave Janet many years ago. Regina dropped her cup of coffee on the floor, realizing she was looking at the woman in the pictures with Charlie.

She excused herself from the table and wept bitterly in the ladies room for nearly fifteen minutes. Vowing to take revenge on them for what they've done to Janet and Charlie, she knew her first move was to meet Maria Richardson in person and set her mind at ease.

***

Later that month she went back to Erie for the first time since that fateful day. After knocking on Maria's front door, she took a glance at her sister's former house next door. No one has purchased the house since the murders. Who can blame them?

Naturally Maria was quite surprised to meet Regina, and after getting over the initial shock, she eagerly invited her into her home. They sat together talking across her kitchen table while sipping on a cup of coffee. Pictures of Charlie, Maria, Janet and Mike were all over the house; vacations, kids birthdays, backyard barbeques. A house that normally was a fun place to be was now so hollow. Maria was all there was left of many years of wonderful memories of days long since gone. There were so many ghosts in this house, and many nights Maria cried herself to sleep – wondering if anything that she'd experienced was real, or was the husband she knew a cruel man. A man cruel enough to murder his next-door neighbor.

After explaining to Maria everything that she'd found out and what she saw for herself, Regina quietly passed a thick file of paperwork across the table to her. She continued to sip her coffee, watching Maria's reactions very intently. Regina's heart went out to her, for clearly Charlie was a very good man. She herself also felt horrible, for Maria shared with her that Regina had a nephew, David, whom she would never know. There was so much tragedy, all because of one man. It wasn't fair.

"He did this? He...*murdered* my Charlie?" Maria stammered, finally picking her head up from the file. Tears were streaming down her face.

"Yes he did Maria, I'm sorry," Regina began. "From what you've told me about your husband and his penchant for practical jokes, I'd say Mike used him as a fall guy. Mike also gave a statement to the police that my sister was on medication because she had a heart condition. Mike is a doctor, and if anyone could figure out how to make all this happen and go undetected in a coroner's report it's him. From start to finish, Mike set up this entire scenario."

"Well the bastard must be punished!" Maria snapped, slamming her fist on the kitchen table. "He took away the only man I've ever loved! I had to sell our business, my friends hardly visit me anymore and my children hate their father all because of that son of a bitch!"

She clearly was angered, and quickly stood to grab the telephone when Regina stopped her.

"Maria, wait! I want you to listen to something first. I've got an idea of how to handle this. Before you call the police I'd ask that you hear me out."

Maria sat down, and together the two of them discussed Regina's plan. For nearly four hours they plotted how they were going to give a fitting payback to the man who tragically changed all their lives forever.

Reciprocity of evil had taken shape inside the Richardson home that day.

***

Their plan had been carried out. Regina stood over Mike's trembling body defiantly, knowing that she'd given a swift and proper justice for Janet and Charlie. The grandfather clock in the upstairs hallway struck half past one.

"I hope you rot in hell, you son of a bitch!" she said, whispering in his ear.

Regina spat in Mike's face and placed the knife she used to murder Jasmine in his right hand. She took off her latex rubber gloves and flushed them down the toilet on the second floor. She changed her clothing, grabbed a light blue duffel bag filled with the tattered white dress and the Jack-in-the-Box and walked defiantly past a trembling Mike, right out the back door.

The storm had finally settled. All clear.

Regina walked to an alley and got into her Honda Accord. She took a deep breath and hit speed dial on her cell phone, holding it to her left ear as she started the car.

"Hello."

"Maria, it's me. I just wanted to let you know that justice has been served, just as we planned."

"Thank you dear......for giving me back my Charlie."

"You're welcome. Sleep easy, Maria. The devil has been given his due."

"Your sister was a wonderful person Regina......she was just like you."

Regina started to cry.

"Thank you, and God Bless you." She hung up the phone.

Regina reached into her duffel bag and came out with her mirror, the same one she received from *her* adoptive parents as a child. The design on the back was similar to the one Janet was given, only it had the infant neatly dressed in a light blue robe as it peacefully laid on the cloud with its guardian angels attending to it. The clothing of the woman hovering above was still black, and she still had a look of pain in her face, but the angels looked different than the ones on Janet's mirror.

As Regina peered into the mirror a bright light came from it, and Janet's image was looking back at her, smiling.

"Thank you, silly-nilly," Janet said.

"What are sisters for, girly-whirley?" Regina replied.

Regina took off and headed down towards Interstate 295, then exited on I-55 for her long trip back to Saint Louis. She never returned to Wheaton again, and there was no need to, for she was ready to place all of this behind her and move on with her life, every bit as much as Maria was now able to move on with hers.

Epilogue

Father's Day, 2004

The rain continued to come down as David waited calmly outside the sanitarium. He bundled himself up in his trench coat, tying the sash firmly around his waist and pulling up his collar to cover his neck.

His heart felt heavy. Another visit with his father and still no real communication between the two of them. He believed that his father would never recover, that he would always be locked away in his padded cell with nothing or no one to be there with him again. Another miserable Father's Day has gone by. David wasn't sure if his dad understood anything or even was aware that he was there. He started to sob.

Adam pulled the car into the sanitarium driveway. David ran through the pouring rain and got into a Blue 2004 Mercury Grand Marquis, running his fingers through his hair trying to dry off. Adam patiently waited for him to settle himself; he could tell this was yet another emotional visit with his dad. He reached over and took David's hand, kissing it gently.

"Are you alright, sweetie?" Adam said, caressing David's fingers.

"Yes, I'm fine," David replied.

Adam put the car in drive and they headed for Chicago, where they've lived for the last few years so David could be close to his father. Adam found a job teaching at the University of Chicago, and David was working at the Northern Trust Bank in the Loop, where he was recently promoted to Director of Economic Research.

Neither man spoke for nearly half the trip. David sat in the passenger seat staring out the window, watching the rain continue to pour. Adam waited patiently, holding his hand for moral support. God knows what was running through David's mind right now.

"Didn't go well, did it?" Adam asked, finally breaking the silence.

David shook his head. "I don't know what to make of him. It's like he's become someone else. He's made no progress since he's been in there. None at all."

David turned and looked at Adam. "He actually spoke this time, though. Real words. Only thing is I have no idea what he was trying to tell me."

Adam seemed amazed. "Wow...well, that's progress, don't you think?"

"I suppose...if you call singing nursery rhymes progress."

"Nursery rhymes?" David didn't respond. For several minutes there was an uncomfortable silence. Eventually Adam could no longer resist.

"So...which one was it?"

David took his time.

"He said: London Bridge is Falling Down, Falling Down, Falling Down, London Bridge is Falling Down, My Fair Lady."

About the Author

David T. Boyd was born and raised in Chicago, Illinois, but now lives in Brooklyn, New York. Falling Down is his first release. Mr. Boyd graduated from St. Ignatius College Preparatory in Chicago, received his Bachelor of Arts in English from SUNY Empire State College and is completing his MFA in Creative Writing at The City College of New York. Besides writing, David loves to exercise, discuss politics and tell everyone why Chicago is the center of the universe. Be sure to visit his website - www.davidtboyd.com.

About the Author

www.ingramcontent.com/pod-product-compliance
Lightning Source LLC
Chambersburg PA
CBHW020140150626
46552CB00021B/934

* 9 780983 248422 *